PRAISE FOR THE FRAGMENT OF MY...

Chosen by Kelly Jensen as ... ooks in Verse" (*Book Riot,* March ...

"An amazing story of loss, love, growing up, and forgiving.... [it] speaks to anyone who has ever asked the questions *Who am I?* and *Who will I become?"* —Jacqueline Woodson

"On rare occasions one reads a book that is just plain touching, pulling the reader in and allowing one to feel what the character feels.... [This] tenderly written book is definitely for the adopted teen but can be enjoyed by all others." —*VOYA*

"Strong feelings are conveyed in few words.... A special book filled with insight." —Claire Rosser, *KLIATT*

"Wonderfully written, often funny, always alive and honest, this brave book... speaks to the outsider and the searcher in all of us." —Adam Bagdasarian

"Kearney uses poetry uniquely to access and express Lizzie's innermost hopes and desires.... A real balance of personal exploration as an adoptee and new teenage emotions creates a powerful blend in a warm character ready to connect and sustain that bond to readers.... A first-rate offering." —*Kirkus Reviews* (starred)

"This tender, wonderfully written story... draws the reader into a world that is both real and revelatory.... No one will ever again wonder why adoptees of all ages long so fiercely to know their biological parentage." —Norma Fox Mazer

"Lovely and insightful, moving and thought-provoking, and a joy to read.... I couldn't put it down." —Adam Pertman

"Lizzie's questions about her identity, about her birth parents' relinquishment of her, and about her connection to family history demonstrate how a particular issue can become a lens through which experience is viewed, and they're questions asked by many, whether adopted or not." —*ALAN*

Also by Meg Kearney

OTHER BOOKS ABOUT LIZZIE McLANE

The Girl in the Mirror:
A Novel in Poems and Journal Entries (2012)

When You Never Said Goodbye:
An Adoptee's Search for Her Birth Mother
A Novel in Poems and Journal Entries (2017)

POETRY FOR ADULTS

An Unkindness of Ravens (2001)
Home By Now (2009)

BOOKS FOR CHILDREN

Trouper (2013)

THE SECRET OF ME

Meg Kearney

A Karen and Michael Braziller Book
PERSEA BOOKS/NEW YORK

for Mom, Dad, Marion, and Sean

Grateful acknowledgment is made to the following authors and publishers whose works are included in this volume:

Hayden Carruth, "The Cows at Night" from *From Snow and Rock, From Chaos,* copyright © 1973 by Hayden Carruth. Reprinted by permission of New Directions Publishing Corp.

Lucille Clifton, "Homage to My Hips" from *Two-Headed Woman,* copyright © 1980 by Lucille Clifton. Reprinted by permission of The University of Massachusetts Press.

Cornelius Eady, "Victims of the Latest Dance Craze" from *Victims of the Latest Dance Craze,* copyright © 1986 by Cornelius Eady. Reprinted by permission of the author.

Donald Hall, "Names of Horses" from *Old & New Poems,* copyright ©1990 by Donald Hall. Reprinted by permission of Houghton Mifflin Co. and the author.

Anne Sexton, "Cinderella" from *Transformations,* copyright © 2001 by Anne Sexton Estate. Reprinted by permission of Houghton Mifflin Co.

Copyright © 2005 by Meg Kearney

All rights reserved. No part of this publication may be reproduced or transmitted in any form or by any means, electronic or mechanical, including photocopy, recording, digital, or any information and retrieval system, without prior permission from the publisher.

Requests for permission to reprint or to make copies, and for any other information, should be addressed to the publisher:

Persea Books, Inc.
277 Broadway
New York, New York 10007

Library of Congress Cataloging-in-Publication Data
Kearney, Meg.
    The secret of me / Meg Kearney.
p. cm.
"A Karen and Michael Braziller Book."
Includes bibliographical references.
ISBN 0-89255-322-7 (alk. paper)
1. Adoption—Juvenile poetry. 2. Teenage girls—Juvenile poetry.
3. Adopted children—Juvenile poetry. 4. Children's poetry, American.
I. Title.
PS3611.E2S43 2005
813'.6—dc22
2005015578

Book design by Rita Lascaro
Typeset in Stone Serif
Manufactured in the United States of America. Printed on acid-free paper.
Third paperback printing, 2017

CONTENTS

THE SECRET OF ME

No one ever keeps a secret so well as a child.
—from *Les Misérables*, Victor Hugo

HOW I ARRIVED

I was five months old by the time I arrived.
It was like a slow, sea-sick ride in the hull of a boat.
It was like having a fever, thinking the world
was blurred and distant, and voices came in
waves. Someone must have held me, sometimes.
Someone must have picked me up when I cried.
Did I have dreams? Did I drink that powdered
milk without a fight? By the time I arrived I had
a name. I had teeth. My legs bowed like a wishbone. I could stretch my knees behind my head.
I was like The New Thing my parents had ordered
from a catalog after lots of shopping around. But
they were puzzled. None of the dresses they'd bought
were my size. No shoes fit. And what, they whispered,
was that little point on her right ear? Why does
she bend like Gumby? Has there been some mistake?
Is this the daughter they promised to send us?

FAMILY PORTRAIT

I'm fourteen and already taller
than Mom (whose hair,
she says, is *not* red—it's
"auburn"). Soon I'll be
taller than my brother Bob
and my sister Kate (they're
the two blondes in our
family), and Dad, too,
whose hair is mostly gray
with a tiny bit of red poking
through. Mom says he
wears the map of Ireland
on his face. Blue-eyed
Bob says I'm an alien.
I throw my answer back
at him like a rotten egg:
At least *I* have brown
eyes like Mom and Dad!
(Theirs are really "hazel.")
Then the man at the photo
studio poses us five
standing under a fake tree
with a fake park
in the background.
He looks through his
camera and then peers
around it, looking right at
me. Where'd they get you
from, he laughs—
the meter reader?
Everybody kind of looks
at each other and laughs,
too, including me, but
I know my smile looks real
fake after that.

TWO MOTHERS

I have two mothers
but not like Toshi
who has two mothers

who live with her
in New Hook and brag
about how much

she looks like one
and acts like
the other. I have two

mothers, but only
know the second
one. My first
mother loved me

so much
she gave me away.
I wonder if it bothers

my mother, the one
who took me in, that
I don't look like her.

I wonder if she ever
worries that my other
mother will want me

back. I wonder if she
ever thinks of me, my
other mother. I hope

no one ever loves me
as much as she did.
What kind of love is that?

EMPTY LIST POEM

Things I Love So Much
I Could Give Them Away:

WHAT I REMEMBER: SUMMER

Visiting Aunt Marge on Long Island in July,
bonfires at Sandy Point Beach, marshmallows,
Uncle Rob saying my name, Lizzie McLane, and singing
"Danny Boy" with an Irish accent,
staying up late

Swimming with Kate and Bob
in Gram's pool—Marco Polo and swan
dives—then checkers in the sun, cream
soda, sunscreen and sun burns

Mom sitting with her easel and paints
in the backyard, the crabapple tree
posing for her,
Gram's zucchini bread

Catching fireflies with Toshi, Jan, and Cathy
in my backyard, the four of us sleeping out
in Bob's old Boy Scout tent that smelled like our basement,
our lemonade stand, picking black caps,
playing kick-the-can, flashlight tag

And every August 18: my birthday party, chocolate
cake, or carrot cake with cream-cheese icing, candles,
presents wrapped like candy, me always wondering
if my first mother remembered what day it was.

SELF-PORTRAIT

My face is a sky full
of freckles. My eyes are brown
earth, ringed by blue
water. My legs are parallel

roads heading off into
the distance. My feet,
two fish; toes and fingers
root vegetables God pulled

from a garden. Dad says
my arms are "statuesque,"
my hair one long tangle
of well-done curly fries.

A tiny hill rises
like a surprise from
the upper ridge of my
right ear. A pinky-shaped

scar points toward my
belly-button, which reminds me
of a little dry well. My heart is
a nest where the people

I love live. When the bad
dreams come like wild storms
to drench my nest with rain,
bash it with hail, smash it

against my ribs, I curl
up in bed like an unborn
baby. I can't sleep for fear
somebody is going to fall.

WHAT I WANT

I want my own room
I want to hit a baseball like a boy does
I want just one cute boy named Peter to notice
I want math to become extinct
I want Gram to quit drinking
I want girl hips (down from 12 to size 6)
I want straight hair
I want to play the guitar
I want a midnight curfew
I want to know how to French kiss
I want to drive a car, any car
I want to own that car
I want to know someone who looks like me
I want Dad's heart to be strong again
I want a stereo in my room and endless music
I want to be sixteen
I want a house with its own library
I want a million-dollar gift certificate to the mall
I want Peter to ask for my phone number
I want my own phone
I want to be pretty
I want to see my name on the cover of a book
I want to know who my other parents are
I want to drive and keep driving
until I find them.

THE SENSE OF SMELL

Cathy said newborn babies can tell their own mother's
milk from any other mother's milk just from the smell.
She said she read it in a book, how they took all these
newborn babies and lined them up on their backs
and put a bowl of their own mother's milk on one side

of their heads and somebody else's mother's milk
on the other side and every baby's head turned toward
its own mother's milk, every time. *"Imagine that,"* Cathy
said. She's adopted, too. She never tasted her mother's
milk, either. "But," she said, "I'd know it if I smelled it."

READING MY POEM
"WHAT I WANT" TO MOM

Last night I called Mom into my room, sat her down
on the edge of my bed. I'm going to read you a poem,

I said, holding my piece of paper so tight I nearly
ripped it in half. My palms were sweaty and I was all

fidgety, like a first-grader in a school play. Her face was
an open window with the sun streaming in, and I stood

in its light. Then I read her the poem and the window
closed. The room went dark. There are just some things

you're not supposed to say to your parents. But
I can write them down. I won't stop writing them.

THE BROKEN PLACE

If you've been wondering where I've been,
I can't tell you. All I'll say is you can't
follow me there. It's the kind of dark

that's never seen light; it's the kind of dark
you're born into, the kind that drags you
back into it again and again like a monster

that sees you walking by its cave and snatches
your arm and pulls you in. You know it's
going to happen, but you walk by that cave

anyway, and before you know it you're feeling
your way along some tunnel, and you keep
falling down and your whole body feels

like it's made of broken glass. Do you know
a place like that? When you get tired you sit
on the floor with your back against the wall.

Welcome back, welcome home, hisses
the monster. Sometimes you stroke its slimy
spine so maybe it'll be nice to you; maybe it

will keep its mouth shut; maybe it'll let you
out soon. Who *is* the monster, you ask? Let's say
it's one of the few creatures on earth who knows

my secret. (*Oh, that's not true! spits the monster
from the cave. Everyone knows you're damaged
goods. Everyone knows you were a mistake before*

you were born.) Can't that Monster ever shut up?
Hey, you didn't hear that, did you? Well,
don't believe a word that monster says.

IRISH CHOWDER

"Something's strange about this
clam chowder," says Bob one night
at dinner. "That's 'cuz this is *Irish*
chowder," answers Kate, who spent
all afternoon making it. "Delicious!"
says Mom, raising her spoon in the air
like a trophy. "Where's the clams?"
Bob asks and Dad starts humming
"Who Threw the Overalls in Mrs.
Murphy's Chowder," a song from one
of the million Irish CDs in Dad's
collection. "Oh *Dad!*" Kate and Mom
and I say together. I know all the words
to this song, and to "When Irish Eyes
Are Smiling," "Danny Boy," and too
many more I'm embarrassed to list.
One of my favorites is "When New
York Was Irish" by Terence Winch,
a guy who plays the accordion and is
almost young compared with
the Clancy Brothers and the Flanagan
Brothers and all those old guys Dad
likes. "There are no clams in Irish
chowder," says Kate. "Just potatoes."
Dad has what they call an Irish
sparkle in his eye when he tells Kate
how much he likes the soup. "You get
your skills as a cook from your
grandmothers," Mom says. "Right,"
says Dad, "just like Lizzie gets her way
with words from me—it's an Irish
trait, you know, Lizzie." "Yeah," says
Bob, "just like that weird superstition
about having to come back in the same
door you went out." Dad gives Bob
a wink, then goes on talking to me.

"Just think of all the great Irish writers,"
he says. "James Joyce, Yeats, Robert
Burns . . . " "Robert Burns was Scottish,
Dad," I say, "but don't forget Seamus
Heaney! He won the Nobel prize,"
I add. "Of course, Heaney!" Dad agrees,
reaching for bread. "So, why no clams?"
Bob asks again. Kate rolls her eyes. Then
Dad and Bob start singing the overalls
song again which makes Mom and even
Kate laugh. I laugh, too, though I'm
thinking about how it could be that
Kate got her cooking skills from *both*
of our grandmothers when Gram
is the only one we've ever known,
and how Dad said my love of words
has to do with being Irish, when
we don't know if I'm really Irish or
not. Bob and Dad laugh when they
finish their song and then Bob says,
"Okay, back to this Irish clam chowder . . . "
Kate looks like she's about to
dump her bowl in Bob's lap. I study
her strawberry-blond hair and blue eyes
and think, Yeah, she could be Irish. So
could I. But not Bob. Definitely not.

WHAT HAPPENED TO CATHY (AND ME) ON THE PLAYGROUND IN THIRD GRADE

I was like that man I saw wavering in the street
as if the sky and the sidewalk were both calling
his name and he didn't know which to answer.
My mouth still tasted like lunch: bologna, mustard,
and mayonnaise on wheat bread. Tang. I stood there,
not able to move forward, not able to walk away.
I could hear what that blond girl was saying, could
see her in Cathy's face, taunting, *Your mother didn't*
want you. She didn't even love you. That's why she
gave you away.

      What happened next is kind of crazy.
It was like another, stronger girl named Lizzie took
over. I could smell my own sweat; my heart was
beating like a marching band. Jan said later she knew
we were meant to be friends when she saw me make
a bee-line for that girl. I didn't say a word, just punched
her in the stomach. She crumpled like paper. There
we were, out on the playground, nobody more stunned
than me, and not one teacher, not even the principal,
acted like he saw me do it, or asked me why.

MY NEW "BEST FRIEND"

Dad took me to his office today so I could type
my poems on his fancy computer. Ms. Rios,
the new secretary, shook my hand, looked me

right in the eye. She wore an egg-colored suit
and Chanel No. 5, just like Mom. "Is this your
daughter?" she asked. When I smiled and Dad

smiled, she said, putting her hand on my arm,
"I knew it right away! You look just like your father."
I laughed like I just got away with something.

"You're her new best friend," he tells Ms. Rios,
"You're one of the few people to ever say that."
She pretends to look shocked. First I wonder,

why doesn't he tell her it's okay that I don't *really*
look like him? Why doesn't he ever say,
"Lizzie's adopted"? How come we talk about

that at home, but never anywhere else? Is it
such a bad thing? How come it has to be a secret?
Then I remember what happened to Cathy that

day on the playground in third grade, and I think
Oh. Maybe Dad's just trying to protect me. Maybe
being adopted is a secret he's helping me keep.

WORD PICTURES OF KATE & BOB

Kate's hands are as soft as sifted flour.
Bob's are tough as a football, and tan
like one, too. Kate's eyes are the blue
of a distant mountain, but Bob's are bright
blue, just like Gram's pool. Kate is bread,
soup, blueberry pie. Bob is pizza, cookies,

barbeque potato chips. When I look at Kate,
I see a tall oak tree, deer resting
underneath. When I look at Bob, I see a red
convertible with its top down and a big
furry bear behind the wheel. Sometimes
Kate sounds like an Irish ballad—a fiddle,

a bagpipe, music so sad it doesn't need
the words. But more she sounds like a waltz—
an accordion and a mandolin and your foot
tapping and she grabs you by the hand
and swirls you into a dance and you don't ever
want it to stop. Bob usually sounds like a rock

band, all electric guitar and pounding drums.
Sometimes he's a corny love song, like "I Want
You and My Hot Tamales Too" or "Love Me
Like a Fish and I'll Love You Like a Worm."
"Whattaya got against worms?" says Bob,
tickling my feet while Kate holds me down

on the living room rug till I yell "I love
worms!" Then Kate lets go and they laugh
real hard until I call them a couple of flying
monkeys (like the ones in *The Wizard of Oz)*
and disappear out the back door before
they can say *There's no place like home.*

SLUMBER PARTY

We're lounging in my room like slugs,
Cathy and me slung on our bellies across
the beds, Deb on the blue shag rug, Jan
in the bean-bag chair, Toshi on the giant
stuffed bear I won at the county fair
when I was ten. Eleven candles light
the room, making Jan's hair into platinum-
blond, butter-colored spikes. Barb kicks off
her sandals as she wanders in (she was
probably in the bathroom, weighing herself

again), snatches a pillow off Kate's bed, flops
down on the rug next to Deb. "What'd I miss?"
We all look at Toshi, who shrugs, says
carefully, "Robert wants to do the wild thing."
"He *what?* Oh!" Barb says too loud.
"Tell him to take a long walk off a short
pier," says Jan, rolling up her T-shirt
sleeves, showing off her muscular
shoulders, like she's about to kick Robert's
butt. Cathy giggles, twirling her braids.

"Don't give it up, girlie! I won't, not for Max,
not for nobody." Cathy says. "But you hardly
see Max since he moved to D.C.," I point out.
"Is it true love? Like, are you gonna get
engaged?" asks Deb. Toshi rolls her eyes.
"You've been watching too many soap
operas, girl," she laughs. "You better
use protection if you do it," says Jan,
and the room goes quiet for a second.
"Talk about pressure, my parents are

pressuring me about college already,"
says Barb, who's now lying on her side
doing leg lifts like she's a model on some
exercise show. (She wishes.)"Me too,

can you believe it?" asks Cathy. Toshi looks
relieved at the change of subject. "It's easy
for you and Lizzie," says Barb. "You've
known what you want to be since you
were born." I'm playing with the three
candles on the table next to my bed,

the ones that stand for me and my two
mothers. Jan and Cathy and I don't talk
about adoption stuff unless we're alone.
"Can you go to college to be a poet?"
Deb asks me and Jan laughs. "She's already
a poet. Teaching herself outta all these,"
she says, waving her arm toward the wall
of books across the room. "What she needs
to learn is how to make money, or else
she's gonna be a starving artist."

I'm already picturing myself at a desk
made of plywood in a Greenwich
Village apartment. "Yeah, unlike Jan,
I don't have talent for fixing cars. I think
I'd better find a day job," I say. "We'll all
live in Manhattan," says Toshi, excited now.
"Cathy'll have her restaurant right down
the street from our apartment. We'll all eat
there every night! And after, me and my
band will perform—before we cut

our first CD and go on tour—and Lizzie
will be this famous writer, Deb will have
her own TV show, Barb, you'll be this
amazing model, and Jan—"You got all
of our lives planned out?" Jan shakes her
head, "Well, not mine." Jan eases herself up
and out of the chair. "Who wants popcorn?"
she asks, already heading out the door.
We all leap up to follow. "No butter,
okay?" Barb shouts. The rest of us laugh.

WHAT I REMEMBER: FALL

Mom carrying a box of sweaters down the attic stairs,
picking apples at Ryan's Farm, hiking in Vermont
with my family (those red and yellow and orange leaves
like a painting), tomato sauce simmering on the stove,
Halloween—I was an old witch, a tree, Pocahontas—

Frost on the tomatoes, cinnamon buns, new school shoes
and jeans and the sweater with Emily Dickinson on the front,
covering text books with brown paper cut from shopping bags,
Canada geese flying over the house and landing in Rothenberg's
Pond, pumpkins, men at the store wearing hunting jackets.

The faces of all those men. I didn't look like any of them.

THE WAVE

When Dad gets sick it's like we've all been hit
by this huge wave that none of us saw
coming, even though we know there's always

a wave out there somewhere, maybe heading
our way. Then Dad's in the hospital and the rest
of us are shaky and kind of dazed, except

Mom. After Dad's heart attack, after his stroke
and after the infection in his heart that meant
he had to be in the hospital for three whole

months, Mom never cried once, not even when
the ambulance pulled up our driveway or when
the paramedics carried Dad out our front door

on a stretcher. Times like that she never gets crazy
with worry like us kids—she doesn't paint,
either—she spends every day at the hospital

and then comes home and talks on the phone
with doctors and Gram and my aunts and all
the people who call to find out how he's doing.

When Kate and Bob and I go to see him, he looks
so happy when we walk in the door, even if
he feels real bad and has tubes coming out of his

arm—he gives us all this huge smile as if
he's really in a hotel room and we're all on
vacation. Now since his open heart surgery—

Dad calls it his "valve job" because they replaced
one of his old heart valves with a plastic one—
he says he has a new life and plans to be around

for a long, long time. Still, every night I say
a prayer for Dad's heart. Every night I pray
that another wave isn't heading this way.

THE PHONE CALL STORIES

Just like Kate and Bob, I've always known I was adopted.
It was just how things were—I thought *all* kids were
adopted until I was four, and Mrs. Dunn next door was
pregnant and I asked Mom who she was going to give her
baby to. What other people think is strange is
normal to us. Like in my family, there's no such thing as
stories about where Mom was when she went into labor, how
Dad rushed her to the hospital and then paced the waiting
room, if we cried or what we weighed when we were born,
no surprise announcement from the doctor, "It's a girl!"
Instead of birth stories, we have phone-call stories...

When the Foundling Home called Mom and Dad
the first time, they were leaving for vacation—
their suitcases were already in the car. Mom said
they took that vacation money and bought a crib,
a dresser, baby girl clothes (the woman in the store
helped them pick the right sizes for a six-month-
old), bottles & formula, and lots of diapers. Then,
they drove to Manhattan instead of Maine, trying
to decide what to name the baby. *With Kate, we needed
a crash course on how to be parents*, Mom said.
We hadn't been that happy since our wedding day.

When the Foundling Home called Mom and Dad
the second time, they were outside in old ratty
T-shirts and shorts, painting the house while Kate
threw toys out of her playpen into the grass.
*I think our faces were still speckled with green
paint when we arrived to pick up Bob*, Mom said.
*Good thing Kate looked clean and well-fed, otherwise
they might have taken one look at us and changed their
minds!* Then they had to go buy diapers for a three-
day-old, little boy clothes, and special formula,
'cause he was allergic to just about everything,
including milk, the Foundling people said.

Three years had gone by when the Foundling Home called Mom and Dad for the last time. They said, "You wouldn't be interested in one more, would you?" They said, "We have a baby girl here who we think would fit right in...and her mother has asked that she have siblings, and not grow up here in the City." So Mom and Dad packed up Kate and Bob and they all drove down to get me. On the way, they voted on what to name me, even though I was five months old and already had a name. Mom said that when she told the case worker that they'd decided to name me Elizabeth, the woman dropped her pen and cried, "It's a miracle! That's the name her mother gave her!"

CATHY'S STORY

"I wasn't easy to give away, girlie,"
Cathy says one night in my
room like she's in some kind of
swoon over a boy, only she's not.
Cathy is half-black, half-white,
and in a swoon over some woman
in a photograph she tells everyone
is her real mother. Her dead mother.
Cathy sinks into the pile of stuffed
animals on my bed, looks up
at the glow-in-the dark stars
on my ceiling. "Where did I belong,
except with her?" she says to me,
knowing I'll play along, knowing
I know the difference between fact
and truth. "Maybe she was a famous
chef, like I'm gonna be, and she died
fat and happy." Cathy presses the photo
to her heart. She carries it just about
everywhere, sleep-overs and parties.
Only Jan and Max and I know it's
not really her mother. Cathy has no
idea who that beautiful black woman
in that frame is, but she loves her.
She misses her, wishes she didn't have
to die. "It's a sad story," Cathy says.
"But who's gonna say it's not mine?"

JAN TELLS HER STORY

My dad taught me how to tune
an engine, how to change a tire

and how to tell just by looking
in a man's eyes whether he's

going to cheat you or not. My dad
taught me how to say some stuff

in Spanish, like *Thank you* and
How much for that car? Mom's

always working at the law
office, doesn't have much time

to talk. So it's Dad I talk to about
boys. After school I walk down

to the shop and talk to his legs
sticking out the bottom of somebody's

Honda, and ask about whether or not
it's okay if boys try to kiss me on

the first date, whether boys really
like girls who wear make-up,

'cause I don't. I even talk with him
about being adopted. You know,

wondering things. Like why
my birthmother never calls me.

She could, if she wanted. She never
even sent me a birthday card. Dad says

she cares about me enough not to
"interfere" in my life. I think she doesn't

want me interfering in *hers*. Maybe
someday I'll call *her*, let her know

that the best thing she ever did was
give me up, give me to my dad.

THE BROKEN PLACE II

Sometimes it's a well I fall into—no,
it's more like a sinking, a slide, then
I'm at the bottom. The sides are slick,
impossible to climb. But that's okay.
I don't have the energy to pick myself
up, climb my way out. I just sit there
shivering until someone calls my name:
Elizabeth, I need you, Mom might call
from the kitchen, and I'll stand up.
Elizabeth, she'll say again. Sometimes
it sounds as if she's singing, and I float
right out of there.

PARENTS NIGHT AT NEW HOOK HIGH SCHOOL: THE UNCENSORED REPORT

I'll bet our school is the only one in the country that has
one hundred percent attendance on Parents Night.
Even after they've met with our teachers, hardly

any parents want to leave—most are drinking
coffee and munching brownies in the cafeteria,
looking really weird sitting at the tables where we

have lunch every day. New Hook is an "artsy-fartsy"
town, says Mom (perfect for her, since she's
a painter) where people care about "what counts,"

like trees and endangered owls. I think most adults
here got stuck in the 1960s, when people still wore
tie-dyed shirts and hitch-hiked and went camping

without tents and believed in a lot of that hippie
love stuff. For the most part, I guess that's a good
thing, but Parents Night is a torture that should end

after grade school, not follow you into ninth grade
because all the parents think it's good for them to be
"involved" in our education. My attitude about this

is a challenge, Dad says (then laughs) because I'm
supposed to write a story about it for our school
paper. Okay, one fact I should correct: not every

parent is here—one of Toshi's moms, Isabel
(she lets us call her that) is a nurse and has to work,
but Jane, her other mom, is over near the big shiny

coffee urn with a bunch of other parents. I saw Peter
and Robert standing there earlier, which was weird
since I doubt they drink coffee. Now the two of them

are scarfing down cookies and laughing, looking like
trouble. What are they up to? Dad said I'd get side-
tracked on this story, watching the boys. Darn it,

he's always right. Most dads probably are. Speaking
of dads, Barb's isn't here, either. He moved
to Wyoming after Barb's mother divorced him—

but Barb's mom, who with dark wavy hair past her
shoulders is almost as pretty as Barb, is always here
(she's president of the PTA, the New Hook Bank,

and the Mothers Who Work Out and Drink Green
Tea Club) with Barb's stepfather, who's the head of
something, too, though I don't know if being Director

of Bustard's Funeral Home is anything to brag about.
Dr. Kingley, Cathy's mom (who's also our dentist)
is leaning across a table talking serious with Jan's

mom, Ms. Mack, a lawyer for poor people. She keeps
looking at her watch, then the door, like she's planning
her escape. Her blond hair is short, but not as short

as Jan's platinum spikes. The librarian, Ms. Thomas,
is following Mr. Kingley around like he's some kind
of hip-hop star not because he can sing or because

he has a *way-cool* pony tail but because he's the guy
who writes all those kids books, like *The Chocolate
Train* and *Bugs for Breakfast*. (Really I don't blame

Ms. Thomas—I follow him around, too, when I go
to Cathy's house.) My parents are talking with Deb's
dad, who owns O'Toole's Pub and is Catholic

like us, though he only goes to Mass on Christmas.
Deb practically grew up at the bar, drinking Coke,
getting addicted to TV. Her parents are divorced,

too, but they both remarried and all of them live in
New Hook—there's her mom over there (you can
tell from how she sucks in her stomach she teaches yoga)—

she's looking over the herbal teas with Mrs. Woodward,
Peter's mom, who does speech therapy over in Stone
Falls and has a neck so long some people call her

The Giraffe behind her back. Mr. Woodward, who
has short, dark hair and little almost-dimples like
Peter (who's nowhere to be seen, must be hiding

in the boys room with Robert . . . maybe Toshi knows),
just got another cup of coffee and joined Mom
and Dad and Mr. O'Toole over near the desserts.

He probably wants to talk school biz, but for once
Dad isn't talking about school stuff but about some
demonstration that's happening next week to protest

plans to build a cement plant not far from us, on
the Hudson River. "It would be a disaster, a huge
disaster. We have to count on the whole community

to help beat this," I hear Dad saying from the corner
where Cathy, Jan, Deb, Barb, Toshi, and I are huddled
on top of one of the lunch tables, rolling our eyes over

our parents' corny conversations, counting the minutes
until we can go home. Then we hear a loud gasp
from Ms. Thomas, who's peering—what? Into

Mr. Kingley's mouth? Suddenly all of the adults are sticking out their tongues at each other—their tongues are *blue!* (But not Deb's mom's, or Mrs. Woodward's...

they were drinking tea...) Someone rigged it so all the coffee drinkers' tongues turned blue! (Hmmmm, wonder who? Peter and Robert are back, standing

in the corner, almost falling on the floor they're laughing so hard.) And now the parents are starting to laugh, too, though Dad is going into his school administrator

mode, already eyeing Peter and Robert. Hey! I can see my headline now: "Students Die of Boredom While Adults Talk a Blue Streak at Annual Parents Night."

E-LOVE

Today Peter sent me an e-mail:
"Hey U! What up, Lizzie?"
All that was "up" seemed so stale.
I wrote, "Math is making me dizzy!"

I knew when I pushed "send"
it was the dumbest line ever written.
It was either die right then,
or write again, hide that I'm smitten

but sound funny and smart,
like a girl he might want to date.
Writing e-mails is a kind of art.
Should I tell the joke about the ape?

I took a chance: "Was thinking of U . . .
it's what I do when Math makes me blue."

DUMB

Dumb dumb dumb
I said all Sunday night

dumb dumb dumb
I wished with all my might

dumb dumb dumb
I didn't write that line

dumb dumb dumb
giving Peter a sign

dumb dumb dumb
I have a crush on him

dumb dumb dumb
I did it on a whim

dumb dumb dumb
when he didn't write back

dumb dumb dumb
I had a snack attack

dumb dumb dumb
Food makes me feel better

dumb dumb dumb
after writing a dumb letter

dumb dumb dumb
opening my feelings like a door

dumb dumb dumb
(that's what *poems* are for)

dumb dumb dumb
Now that Monday's here

dumb dumb dumb
I just want to disappear

dumb dumb dumb
Instead I have to hope at school

dumb dumb dumb
when I see him I'll be cool

WHAT SISTERS ARE FOR

There's times I don't know what to do or say,
like when I screw up, and feel really bad.
Come on, Kate tells me. *It'll be okay.*

Once at a restaurant called Café Le May,
I tripped and spilled my salad all over Dad.
There's times I don't know what to do or say.

When I'm failing math, which is *every day*,
Bob teases, "You can write, but you sure can't add!"
Come on, Kate tells me. *It'll be okay.*

I was sick one Halloween, but went out anyway,
then threw up in Bob's candy bucket. Was he mad!
There's times I don't know what to do or say—

like when adults joke about "a roll in the hay"
and then laugh too loud—including my own dad!
Come on, Kate tells me. *It'll be okay*—

it usually is, unless I see Peter and Sue at Video Bay
and I'm in my sweats, feeling ugly and sad.
There's times I don't know what to do or say.
Come on, Kate tells me. *It'll be okay.*

FRIENDS

Sometimes you just know when somebody's going to be
your friend. Jan, Cathy, and I knew it the moment

I punched that girl in third grade (I was their
hero, they both said). Toshi and I knew it

the day there was one piece of chocolate cake left
at Deb's tenth birthday party and we decided

to split it. Deb and I knew when our health teacher
talked about alcoholism, and we caught each other's

eye in class, and knew we both knew something
we wished we didn't. (Later we talked about people

in her dad's bar; even later we talked about my
Gram.) Barb and I knew after the first few of the million

PTA meetings our parents dragged us to—we went
from playing hop-scotch and swinging on monkey bars

to smoking our first (and last) cigarette together, out
back of the school. And just yesterday Peter and I knew,

when I was in such a hurry to avoid him (still
embarrassed about that dumb e-mail) and I slammed

my finger in my locker door and dumped all my
books on floor. I let out a shout and a bunch of kids

started laughing. Peter ignored them. He picked
up my books, then said, *Hey, let me see that finger.*

ANOTHER ONE OF US

Shopping with Mom or Dad is like going out
with the mayor. They know so many people
I usually keep count of how many we run into,
which is always a lot, which is why shopping

always takes twice as long as it should. So
Mom and I are in Kelley's Grocery last
Saturday, and here come Isabel and Jane—
Toshi's moms—and I count, *Seven, Eight.*

Toshi isn't with them, so I say hi and then
grab Mom's list and take off toward
the baking aisle. By the time I get back
with a box of brown sugar, they're all

just saying good-bye. Mom and I round
the corner of the cereal aisle, and there's
Ms. Hubbard, one of the newest teachers
in my school. She's holding the hand

of a little Asian girl. "Hello, Mrs. McLane!"
calls Ms. Hubbard, and I think, *Nine.*
Do I count the little girl? Ms. Hubbard
tosses a box of oatmeal in her cart and

heads our way. "I want you to meet
someone special. This is my newly
adopted daughter, Grace. She just arrived
from China." Mom and I both bend

down and say hi to Grace, who's
sucking her thumb and staring at her
little red shoes. She can't be more than
three years old. "You have pretty shoes,

Grace," I say, but she doesn't look up.
Mom stands, touches Ms. Hubbard
on the arm. "She's beautiful, Laura."
Ms. Hubbard beams like a flashlight.

"But please remember," Mom adds,
"Grace is not your adopted daughter.
She is your *daughter*." Ms. Hubbard
looks confused for a second, and then

smiles. "Yes, it's a miracle, isn't it?"
"They're all miracles," Mom answers,
then looks down at me like I'm a winning
lottery ticket. I'm amazed that Mom

actually said that to Ms. Hubbard—part
of me wishes she'd add, "Lizzie's adopted,
too," and part of me is terrified she will . . .
but I know she won't. I notice Grace

staring at my turquoise ring, hold out
my hand for her to touch it. *Well,
I guess you're number 10,* I think.
Welcome to New Hook, Grace.

ADOPT A USELESS BLOB
(SIGNS I'VE SPOTTED)

Adopt a Pet
Adopt a Highway
Adopt a Dragon
Adopt a Dolphin
Adopt a Stream
Adopt a Demon
Adopt a Bat
Adopt a Beach
Adopt a Bird
Adopt a Minefield
Adopt a Manatee
Adopt a Platoon
Adopt a Ghost
Adopt a Rainforest
Adopt an Insect
Adopt a Turkey
Adopt a Bunny
Adopt a Useless Blob

. . . no wonder Mom doesn't want to say
I'm adopted!

CROSSING OUR HEARTS IN THE DARK

It's not enough that Deb's father owns a bar;
at Deb's house he's got a bar in the basement,
with stools that twirl and a refrigerator
full of Dr. Pepper and Diet Coke. Deb likes

to play bartender, and tonight she served
snacks with our sodas: potato chips, M&Ms,
and for Barb, pretzels 'cause they're non-fat.
She cares about stuff like that. Ever since

she came back from being with her Dad
in Wyoming all summer, Barb's seemed
kind of sad, so tonight a few of us are going
out of our way to find out what's up

and make her feel better. Nobody knows
how to come out and ask her, though, so all
night it hasn't come up, and now we're in
our sleeping bags (Deb, Barb, Toshi,

and me) with just flashlights on, moving
their circles of light around like huge
fireflies on the ceiling. "My Mama got
arrested for stealing a flashlight once,"

says Toshi, and we all gasp. "That was before
she met Mom," (that's Isabel—her Mama
is Jane) "when she was still in high school."
"*Wow*," Deb says. "She told you that?"

"Not exactly," says Toshi. "One night the two
of them were having a fight and it kinda
came out." "Holy Cow," I say and Deb says,
"That's how you find out stuff about

your parents—when they're fighting!"
Deb and Toshi make their two flashlight
fireflies fight, ramming them into each other
on the ceiling. "That's how I found out

that my Uncle Rick had been in prison,"
says Deb, and we all say "WHAT?" "Yeah,"
she says, "for selling drugs. My parents never
told me, but one night during a huge fight,

Mom said Dad was just like his lying,
drug-running brother 'the ex-con.' That was
just before they got divorced." "*Geez*,"
says Toshi. "That's *baaaaad*." "And sad,"

Deb says. "I have an uncle I've never
even met!" "Deb, that's really heart-
breaking," I say, thinking about my family
secret. "Most families probably have stuff

like that, stuff they hide," Toshi says.
Barb turns off her flashlight. We pretend
not to notice. "My Dad's a jerk," she says
all of a sudden. There's a few seconds

when none of us say anything, then I say,
"All our parents can be jerks sometimes... "
"No," Barb says. "*Really*. He's seeing some
woman who I swear is barely older than

us, well maybe she's twenty, and she's *married*."
"Aw, crap," says Toshi. "That's no good."
"Yeah," says Barb, "and every single night
I'm there, he's either on the phone talking

real low to her, or he's out somewhere, with
her I'm sure, and he doesn't get home until
real late, like three a.m.! So I'm like, Why did I
bother to come here? That's what a jerk he is!"

she says, then she adds, "Please don't tell
anybody this? Please—" "Don't worry,"
says Toshi. "We'll all swear not to tell any
of this stuff, not about your dad or my

mama or Deb's uncle. Right?" "Cross our
hearts and hope to die," says Deb. "Yeah,
cross my heart," says Barb. "Me too!"
I say, "I'm the world's best secret-keeper."

HISTORY LESSON

"Remember when we were in fifth grade
and the teacher gave us that assignment

to make our family tree?" I ask. Cathy is
on my bed, painting her toenails purple

while I water my rubber tree and Kate's yucca.
"Yeah," she laughs, "Mom and Dad wanted me

to list all of *their* ancestors. I cut pictures
out of *Essence* magazine instead, and glued

them on this piece of cardboard I cut to look
like a tree. What did you do?" she asks.

"It made me so mad, my face must have
turned the color of that nail polish. I turned

in a mini-tree, with just me, Mom, Dad, Bob,
and Kate. Ms. Abbott's eyes about bugged out.

'Where's the rest of your tree?' she said, real
snotty like. I said: 'Struck by lightning.'"

DIFFERENT

There's a family story Kate likes to tell
about how after they got me, Mom
and Dad sat her and Bob down to tell
them some big, BIG news. Mom

was going to have a baby. A baby!
Mom was pregnant with a child
they called "*natural*." "A baby
like you or me is not a 'natural' child,"

Bob always reminds me. "We're called
'*illegitimate*.'" This makes Kate mad
but she goes on, "When Mom called
us, Bob and I thought she was mad

about something, and then we saw
Dad with this huge grin on his face,
and he gave us the news. I saw
they were both nervous, but Mom's face

was lit like Times Square. She asked, 'How
do you feel? I know this way is different
from the way we got you.' And Bob said, 'How
we gonna tell this kid *he's* different?'"

E-LOVE GONE BAD

Peter's been e-mailing me two, three times
a night. We don't talk about anything
special—just school, and cool stuff he finds
on eBay, and college basketball. He thinks

next spring B.U. might make the Final Four.
I say, "No way, S.U.'s gonna cream them."
He writes back, "Wanna bet on the score
or just the winner?" I write, "Orangemen

in overtime by 4 points." "4! So what
does the winner get?" he types back.
A kiss, I think, but say, "Winner's choice, but
U have to be nice." "OK, odds are stacked

against you, Lizzie," he says. Then ruins it
all with "Hey, U got a # for Sue Schmitt?"

FOOD FIGHT

For lunch today Barb ate some carrots, an apple,
and a protein bar. "What's up with that lunch?
You plan to live off that?" asked Jan, her eyes
narrowed like they are when she plays basketball.
Barb looked right at me and said, *"I'm* on a diet."

Jan rolled her eyes, "You're already a size negative
two." Barb fidgeted a little on the bench. "My mom
says" (she waved a carrot in the air like a teacher),
"You can never be too rich or too thin." "Someone
famous said that," I blurted—"Your mom didn't

make that up herself!" "Well, *anyway*, it's true,
you have to be thin if you ever want a boy to like you,"
Barb said, knowing that would make me shut up.
"That's *bull*," said Jan. I looked at my bologna
sandwich, bag of cookies Mom made just for me.

All of a sudden I wasn't very hungry. "Don't listen
to her," Jan said. "Lizzie, you're perfect just the way
you are. If Peter's too stupid—" I held up my hand
for Jan to stop. Cathy shook her head, said, "You
white girls think way too much about this weight stuff."

I got up, tossed what was left of my lunch
in the garbage, and walked out of that cafeteria,
already feeling guilty about throwing out those
cookies (I could have given them to Cathy) but
swearing I'd be a size smaller by Christmas.

THE BOX

Ever since I read that poem to Mom,
the one that went over like a paper
plane on fire, I've been waiting
for the perfect moment to ask her
what it was that scared her, ask
if it's wrong for me to want to find
my birthparents, tell her I need her
to say that searching for them
would be okay. But when Mom
and I are sitting on my bed folding
shirts and jeans and other stuff
that doesn't fit me anymore, I get
all queasy in my stomach, knowing
NOW is the time to ask her, but
feeling afraid of . . . I don't know
what. So I tell her about Shirley
Rooter, the senior girl who's
pregnant and quitting school.
"Oh, that poor child," Mom says.
I tell her even though Shirley's
boyfriend is a jerk, her parents
have been really supportive.
They've got money and they're
gonna help out, so don't worry
about the baby, I explain,
and Mom looks up from folding
what used to be my favorite
nightgown. "I meant poor Shirley—
she's just a child having a child."
"Oh! Right!" I say too fast.
My heart's dribbling like
a basketball under my T-shirt.
"Mom, do you know—
was my birthmother just a child,
too? I mean, was she still in high
school?" Now Mom is smoothing

out a pair of Levi's, straightening
the legs. Without looking up
she says, "Well, Lizzie, we don't
really know." She folds the jeans
like they just came off the shelf
at Macy's. I swear she's blushing
when she says what she's *always*
said: "What we do know is she loved
you, enough to give you to us. Now
here," she says, putting the jeans
in the box and closing the cardboard
flaps. "Be a good girl and take this box.
Put it in the trunk of the car." I open
my mouth, close it. Then I pick up
that box and carry it out to the garage.
I pop the Datsun's trunk and think,
"Be good" meant "Be quiet." I think,
everything we're allowed to say
about being adopted, all we're allowed
to ask, to know, to feel, fits in a little box.
Nothing else is allowed in,
nothing else is allowed out.

LOVE SICK

When our bus pulls up to Peter's stop every morning,
he's always there, throwing snowballs at John Keyes,
or playing Frisbee if it's nice out, or reading a book.

He gets on the bus, and I wave as he walks past me,
and he waves back. Then I see him after second
period. His locker is three down from mine. Before

he started going out with Sue we used to talk as we
turned our combination locks and dug through our
stuff, looking for whatever we needed until lunch.

Now Sue stands between us with her back to me,
sticks to him like mold on bread, flipping her hair
every two seconds like someone's taking her picture.

She's pretty, I'll admit it. And a lot skinnier than
I am. Sometimes Peter manages to say Hi over her
shoulder, and I swear he looks embarrassed. Or maybe

I just want to believe that. And to think I gave him
Sue's phone number. To think I had this crazy idea
that he would ever want to go out with a girl like me.

WHAT I REMEMBER: WINTER

Sledding down Farmer's Hill with a million other kids,
snowsuits, blue mittens, hot chocolate with Jan and Cath
and Toshi in Mom's kitchen, Dad showing us how to build
a fire in our living room fireplace, skating on Rothenberg's Pond,
homework, reading *Jane Eyre* the first time, French toast.

The hat Gram knit me out of rainbow yarn, shoveling
her driveway with Bob and Kate, feeling like an icicle
at the bus stop, the icicles dripping from the edge
of our roof, snow-ball fights, snow forts, snowy mornings
hoping for the phone to ring—Dad's boss saying, No school
today!

Standing at my bedroom window, wondering...
if my birthmother had kept me,
would I have grown up where there's lots of snow,
or a place like Florida, or Mississippi, or Arizona?

SEARCHING SESTINA

It's a cold, snowy day, and so us girls are stuck
eating lunch inside, talking about the history
test we just took and who's going to the dance
next Friday. Toshi and Cathy have dates
(Max is coming from D.C.). Jan's not going.
She thinks school dances are a corny waste

of time. "Hey, Peter's arm is around Sue's waist!"
says Deb. Suddenly my sandwich feels stuck
in my throat. "I hear Peter and Sue are going
out," she whispers. "First time in history,"
Cathy sneers, "that Deb's last to know who dates
who in this freakin' school." "Back to the dance,"

Toshi says. "Who's going? Liz?" "I'm gonna dance
down to the library," I say, "and not waste
another second talking about if I have a date
or not." "I'll go, too," Cathy says, "I'm stuck
in math, and need your help with my history
homework." "History, okay, but if you're going

to ask about math," I laugh, "forget it." We're going
down the hallway alone now, so I don't dance
around what's on my mind: Cathy's history,
how she found her birthparents. "That waste
of a man, that crazy lady, you mean? Dad and I stuck
around that adoption agency, asking for dates,

begging for facts." She looks sad. "The only dates
I know are birth and adoption dates," I say. "It's going
to be long road," Cathy tells me, "You'll get stuck
all the time, with people trying to trip you or dance
their way out of telling the truth, trying to waste
your time, wanting you to give up your history,

your own blood, and not make waves." "My history
is my right, though! It's not just a file full of dates!"
"Right," Cathy says, tossing a wrapper in the waste
basket. "But some people think your going
searching is bad news. They'd rather you dance
yourself outta sight, or sit tight, stuck

and stupid like a good adoptee who's not going
to make trouble." "Too bad," I say. "I can't dance
around it." "It's time," Cathy grins, "to come unstuck."

TABOO SUBJECT

Here's what happens when Bob's got the TV remote control:
the three of us, Kate and Bob and me, sit in the living room
saying "yes" and "no" to whatever shows come up. Bob
figures that even though Kate is the oldest, he's the biggest
(he plays defense on the high-school football team) and I'm

just "Squirt" (a name he should drop now that I'm fourteen
and second-string center on our basketball team) so he should
be in charge of entertainment, meaning TV. Usually Bob lets
Kate watch whatever she wants, as long as it's not a cooking
show, and he mostly lets me watch what I want if I'll bring him

chips, Cokes, and basically be his maid, which is what I'm doing
when he flips to one of those interview shows—a woman has
just been reunited with the grown daughter she gave up
for adoption as a baby—I shout "Yes!" But Bob changes
the channel anyway. "Hey," I say, "I wanted to see that." Bob

shrugs, "Too bad, we don't," and Kate doesn't say a word.
"Why don't you guys ever want to talk about who our birth
parents are?" I say. "Mom and Dad are our parents," Bob says.
"But don't you just want to know where you come from?" I ask.
"Are you Irish? German? Hungarian? Jewish? Was your great-

great grandfather a king, or famous serial killer? Should you
worry about cancer, about losing your mind?" Kate shakes her
head, gets up and heads down the hall toward our bedroom.
She walks like a dancer, I think, a dancer who's sad because
she can't hear the music. "Where's your loyalty?" says Bob,

handing me the remote. I say, "This doesn't have anything
to do with how much I love Mom and Dad." He shrugs again.
"I've got homework, Squirt," he says. "Bob, can't you see,"
I'm almost crying, "It doesn't mean I don't appreciate them!
...*Does* it?" I ask Bob's back as he walks out of the room.

FIVE: HOME GAME

The game's at five o'clock against Stone Falls,
ranked fifth in our division with five more wins
on their record than we've got. Five minutes
into the second half, two things happen at once:
Tanya Murillo fouls out, which means I'll play
center for the rest of the game, and Peter strolls in
to the gym with five of his friends, boys who
usually won't be caught dead watching girl's
basketball. Tanya slaps me five as we trade
places, and I'm embarrassed by my sweaty palms,
my face, which I know is red and not because
I've been running around like she has. *What's
Peter doing here? Where's Sue? Do my feet look
really huge? What if I screw up in front of HIM?*
I nod to M.J., Dalia, Margaret, and Jan (who's
giving me that "Did you see Peter's here?!" look),
and take my defensive position in the middle
of the key. I study the other five girls about to bring
the ball this way—I recognize them all, we've played
them lots of times, and know the name of two:
the red-haired forward, Penny; and the other center,
April, number five and the only other girl as tall as
me. April catches me looking but then the ball's in
play and all eyes are on their guard, dribbling down
court like a pro, watching us in our zone and her own
teammates, waiting for the moment she'll make
her move and pass—then I mostly forget about
Peter in the bleachers 'cause these girls are good
and fast and five points ahead. They score and then
we do—Margaret's one of my guards and I always
seem to find her in the key if I have the ball—she's
a great shot and we start to close that five-point gap
but with less than a minute to go they're still up
one point and that's when I blow it—I foul their guard
Penny as she jumps to take a shot. She and her girls
have all got these grins then, 'cause she hardly misses

from the foul line. We set up at the key and swish, swish, two easy points. We try to score again but there's the buzzer. I feel so bad shaking hands with the other team, though Penny says "Good game" like she means it, and April smiles a real smile, then M.J. and Jan give me a squeeze as we head off the court and who's standing there near Coach Brennan but Peter. Now at least I have an excuse for my red face. "It was a good game, Lizzie," he says. I try to smile but my smile muscles aren't working. He adds, "You and Margaret got a great thing going on offense." He's serious, sweet, and I don't want to know where Sue is—I want to hug him even though I probably smell. Margaret grabs my hand, "Next time," she says, and I say, "Yeah, next time for sure." Coach Brennan booms, "You girls played a great game against a really tough team," then I see Mom and Dad heading toward us with their "We're proud of you anyway" looks. I finally smile, and Peter slaps me a high five. I swear, my hand tingles for a whole week.

WISHING

I wish I were more like Kate. She gets A's
on every report card and hardly has

to study. She doesn't have any freckles,
and tans so easily in the summer, unlike

me. Ever since I was little she let me stay
up late if she was babysitting, and we'd

make popcorn and watch romantic movies.
She makes cooking look fun, and doesn't

seem to care whether she has a boyfriend
or not. She's going to college next fall,

where she says the boys are much more
mature, not like high-school boys. One

day I find her in the kitchen, trying out
a new recipe for pineapple nut bread.

She hands me a wooden spoon and the bag
of walnuts. While I'm stirring I tell her all

about Peter and how I thought he liked me
until he started going out with Sue.

"Peter—you mean Sam Woodward's brother?"
She says "Sam Woodward" like she's saying

"summer vacation" or "chocolate cake." "Yes,"
I sigh. "Well," Kate says, flicking on the oven

to pre-heat, "If he's really Sam's brother, he'll
open his eyes, and see which girl is the real

beauty: the smart, artistic, sensitive Lizzie
McLane." "Oh geez, Kate," I laugh, wanting

to believe every word she says about me,
and about Peter coming around. Just spilling

my guts like that make me feel so much
better. Kate gives me a huge hug and says,

"You know you can talk to me about anything."
Oh, I think, I wish that were really true.

WHAT I REMEMBER: CHRISTMAS

Shopping in New York City with Mom, Dad, Kate, and Bob,
the tree at Rockefeller Center as big as a building, sitting
on Santa's lap in Macy's, hot pretzels with salt and mustard
from the man on the sidewalk, the giant train at the F.A.O.
                                                    Schwarz
toy store, riding in a horse-drawn carriage in Central Park.

Church at dawn on Christmas morning, singing "Silent Night"
and "Glory to the Newborn King," being cold, huddled
between Kate and Bob in the old Chevy's back seat...opening
stockings before breakfast, then presents: the fish tank, Barbie,
a blank book for poems, a pen that writes in invisible ink.

Thinking, Merry Christmas, Other Mother, wherever you are.

BAD NEWS, GOOD NEWS

"I have good news and bad news," Deb
says, digging through her bottomless
purse in the girl's bathroom. Toshi
is behind me, braiding my hair.
"Uh-oh," she says, winking at me
in the mirror. "I'm serious,"
Deb says, pulling out her lipstick.
She waves it in the air like she
just won a prize. "We already
know Max can't make it to the dance,"
I say. "Yeah, Cathy's bummed," Toshi
says. "No, it's got nothing to do
with them! This is news for Lizzie."
Deb's loving this. "Okay, what news?"
I ask. "You want the good news first
or the bad news?" "The bad," I say.
"Good choice, but hold still, " says Toshi.
"This color's called 'Kiss Me You Fool,'"
says Deb, spreading red across her
lower lip, then the upper. "What
do you think?" she asks, stepping back
from the mirror, smacking her lips.
"I think you'd better tell us what's
up," says Toshi, tapping me on
the shoulder, "Hand me a hair tie."
"Well," says Deb, torturing me now.
"After first period I saw
Peter and Sue outside the gym."
"Yeah," Toshi shakes her head, "that's bad
news!" "Why are you telling me this?"
I ask. "Because the good news is,"
Deb pauses to blot her new lips
with a piece of toilet paper,
"they were having a bad-ass fight."

MISTAKES

We're supposed to be helping each other
with math homework, but instead Jan
and Cathy and I are talking about
Shirley Rooter and how A.J. is being
a stupid jerk now that she's pregnant,

and whether or not we ever want kids
of our own. "Wow. Think—all those little
ones running around, lookin' like you!"
says Cathy. "I'd rather be locked up
in prison for murder," says Jan, pouring

us a round of root beer. We're at her house,
where root beer rules. I tell them the story
I heard from Kate about Mom getting
pregnant after they got me, how Bob asked
the question about how to tell that baby

he was different. Jan and Cath get a real
kick out of that. But she lost the baby,
I add, and that was it. "Wow," says Jan.
"You know, I don't think my Mom ever got
over not being able to have kids. Her own,

I mean. She gets weirded out around babies—
like she wants to smother them with kisses,
and run in the other direction at the same time.
Maybe that's why it's hard for her to be—
you know, my mom." Jan sits back down

and stares at her drink. Cathy brings up
Shirley again. "Have you seen that girl?
She's getting bigger by the second."
"Doesn't she know about *condoms*?" I say, feeling
kind of mean. But I'm on a roll, adding, "If I ever

have a baby, it's not going to be by accident.
I'm not going to make a mistake like I was." Cathy
twirls her hair around her pencil. "Now
we're playin' in the dirt, girlie." "She's talking
the truth," says Jan. "We were *all* mistakes."

MORE ADVICE ABOUT SEARCHING

Jan says, What if you found your birthmother
and she rejected you all over again? So risky...

Cathy says, Knowing is better than not knowing,
even if your birthparents end up to be crazies.

Bob says, It's illegal, you know. All that stuff,
like your real birth certificate, is locked up. Forever.

Kate says, Don't go there.

CRAZY LOVE PANTOUM

Peter called me again today
he and Sue are fighting
She always wants her way
he said, It's getting really boring

He and Sue are fighting
at school, on the phone, on e-mail
He said, It's getting really boring
hearing her words cut like nails

at school, on the phone, on e-mail...
That's it, I'm telling her I'm sick
of hearing her words cut like nails,
she's about as sweet as a stick!

That's it, I'm telling her I'm sick,
forget about going to that dance.
She's about as sweet as a stick,
unlike you, Liz. If I had a chance

I'd ask you about going to that dance.
I know we're pals and all, but gee
I like you, Liz. If I had a chance
I'd ask you to go out with me.

I promise, Sue and I are done
(she always wants her way)—
So be my girl, Liz? Will ya, Hon?
Peter called me again today.

A SECRET'S OUT AT DINNER

"Lizzie's got a boyfriend!" Bob announces as we
start to crowd into our little dining room for dinner.
I feel my face go red as the painting on the wall,
one of Mom's abstracts called "Fire Catches Fire."

"BOB," I say, probably kind of annoyed, and Dad
gives me a big smile. "Peter Woodward?" he asks.
I can't believe it—how did he know? I say, "We're going
to the dance, that's all." Kate comes up behind

Bob with a plate of chicken in one hand, and claps
her free hand over his mouth just as he's about to say
something else to torture me. Mom's right behind her
with a basket of bread and a plate of baked potatoes—

"What's this I hear about Lizzie?" she says, and Dad
says, "She's got a boyfriend!" *"Oh Dad,"* Kate and I say
together. We have to laugh then, and Kate lets go
of Bob. After we sit down and say grace, I ask Mom

how her painting is going. She wears her thick hair
in a single braid, and has that look like she's been somewhere
far, far away, and has only come back for a little while.
"It's starting to talk to me," she says. I know that means

it's going really great. Then I ask where Gram is—
I thought she was coming for dinner. Dad asks Kate
to pass the butter, and Mom says, "Gram is tired. She
didn't feel up to it. Maybe tomorrow." I think,

I've heard that before. And it feels, as Bob would say,
like the question just sucked all the fun out of the room.
Then Mom asks me, "So is it Peter? Do you need a ride
to the dance?" I wonder, how come we're all talking

about the one subject I'd rather not? I say, "Yeah, a ride
would be great." Then Dad launches into the story
of the first time he and Mom ever went dancing,
and all that fun comes flooding back to the table.

WHAT TO WEAR TO THE DANCE?
I WORRY AND KATE GIVES ADVICE

Everybody says they're wearing jeans to the dance.
How about my Levis? Do these make me look fat?

My dark denim skirt would show off your long, long legs.
You can borrow it if you want. But no, not fat. Forget that.

Wow, thanks! But my legs are so white. You really think
I'd look all right? I don't want Peter to regret he asked me out.

You look beautiful. Really. And he'd have to be deaf, dumb,
and blind to think that, which I doubt.

You're the best, Kate. But then, what kind of shoes
go with this skirt? Heels? Sandals? I have no shoes!

I'll take you to the mall, your favorite store. Hey,
what are big sisters for? Don't worry about the shoes.

You ARE the best, Kate. So, what next? My lucky shirt?
Is it pretty enough? Does blue go with blue?

This black one fits better. Flatters your dark eyes,
too. Don't worry about Peter. Let him worry about you.

DANCE

Jan decided to come tonight, 'cuz otherwise
we'll all be talking about it and she'll feel
left out. (That's how poor Cath will feel—
she's home, mad 'cuz Max didn't come.) Jan's
standing, arms crossed, over near the DJ, who's
a senior with lots of cool CDs, a cute face,
and a motorcycle she's been dying to ride.
She's got on her black T-shirt, black jeans, black
boots, and that look on her face that means
Don't even think about asking me to dance. But
I know inside she wishes someone would.

Deb and Barb are sharing a water bottle,
their faces all red from dancing. They'll
dance all night with any boy who asks,
or else with each other, because it's
a great way to burn calories. Deb keeps
checking her watch, probably thinking
about what TV show she's missing. Barb
keeps asking if she looks fat in her
size-two jeans. Every time I catch them
looking at me and Peter, they wave
and flash me those green smiles.

It seems Toshi & Robert have been kissing
outside the bathroom about every two
minutes. (Toshi says kisses are all he's
gonna get, at least 'til they graduate.)
Otherwise they're dancing or gobbling Fritos
at the snack table, Robert tapping his foot
to some song only he can hear. He and Peter
have been friends since kindergarten.
They slap their hands together and wink,
and Toshi and I mimic them, making up
some silly handshake and laughing.

Peter was waiting outside the school when Mom dropped me off and he's been holding my hand ever since. At first we both felt pretty shy, like we hadn't been friends all this time, but already we're more relaxed and I think he might try to kiss me before the night's over. I keep worrying that my hands are too sweaty and maybe I should have worn my hair down, but then he smiles at me and for a few minutes I forget about what might be wrong and just feel happy.

HEALTH LESSON

"You people shouldn't be eating all those burgers
and fries and chips," Mr. Massie preaches in health
class—"especially if heart disease runs in your family.
Like you, Peter—didn't you say your father has a bad
heart?" Later, at lunch, Peter and I laugh about how
he nearly choked on his gum when Mr. Massie
said his name. "Yeah, what about *you*?" says Peter, giving
me a jab in the ribs. "Doesn't your dad have a bad heart,
too?" He thinks he has a point. I want to say,
My dad isn't related to me by blood. I don't know
what diseases really run in my family. Instead I say,
"Yeah, that's right. You give up burgers and I will, too."

A MATTER OF LOYALTY

For once it's Bob who brings up the subject.
He's driving me home from basketball
practice, and when he turns down the radio
I know it's Big Brother Chat Time. "So,
Lizzie," he starts, "you've been asking a lot
of questions lately about this adoption
stuff. You know, wanting to know who
your natural mother is and all...."
"Birthmother," I tell him. "I say 'birthmother.'"
"Yeah, okay, birthmother. Well, there's
a reason why we don't talk about it much.
You know, it's kinda like no one talks about
Gram and her drinking. It's this thing
we all avoid, not just because it's easier
that way, but because we don't want to
hurt people. You don't want to hurt Mom
and Dad, do you?" It feels like the car
is spinning in circles, instead of heading
straight down Route 55. Bob just mentioned
Gram's drinking like it was something
he and I had talked about a million times
before. Two taboo subjects in one chat!
Holy Cow, I have to take a gulp out
of my water bottle just to concentrate
on what he's saying instead of the FACT
that he's saying it. "Of course I don't,"
I manage to say. Then I feel some courage
and add, "But why don't we talk about it?
Cathy's parents talk about her being adopted."
"Lizzie, it's obvious that Cathy's adopted,
and it really has nothing to do with that,
with other people or what they think,"
he says. Then he takes a deep breath.
"Okay. Put yourself in Mom and Dad's
shoes. They've given us everything—
they've been nothing but great parents,

you know, as great as parents can be.
Do you want to make it seem like all
they've done for us hasn't been good
enough?" *(I won't cry. I won't.)* "See,
Mom and Dad believe in a really deep way
that you're their *daughter*, not their *adopted*
daughter. We're *their* kids, not their adopted
kids, and that's how they treat us, how they
want everybody else to treat us, to see us.
It's a matter of loyalty, Lizzie. Just
like they're totally loyal to you. If you look
for your natural parents, Mom and Dad
will think they failed somehow. Do you
really want to do that to them?" I feel like
Bob just dribbled a basketball right past me,
scoring before I could even stick my hands
in the air. "Of course not," I whisper.
"Huh? What's that?" He turns down the radio
some more. *"No,"* I say louder, crossing
my arms, holding back my tears. Bob says,
"Good. So whaddya say we go for pizza?"

CATHY'S BEST ADVICE

"Then he switched the subject to pizza!"
I tell Cathy on the phone. "You were
shanghaied," she says. I get up and head
for the dictionary to look that up, even
though I already know it means Bob
tricked me somehow. "Listen—his
heart's in the right place," says Cathy.

"Big brothers are always trying to protect
everybody. It's his job. He thinks he's
protecting your mom and dad, and he
thinks he's protecting you from getting
hurt." (I find "shanghaied." Yeah, Bob
had tricked me all right. Kind of . . .)
"Yeah, well, Cath," I say, "wasn't he just

wanting me to see things the way he does?
He is older than us, and knows a lot. . . . "
"Look," Cathy says. "You know deep down
that searching for your birthmother
isn't wrong. Just the opposite. It's your
birthright. (I like that word, birthright.)
But maybe it's just not the right time.

"You can't even talk about it to anybody
but me and Jan, but you think you're ready
to start writing letters to the Foundling,
calling strangers for help?" (I'm silent.)
"See what I'm saying? The first step
toward searching is telling. Take it from
me. It's only 'cause my dad's adopted

that I had help getting past all that loyalty
stuff, and why he went with me to Michigan
when I searched. You're gonna have to be able
to say to someone outside of our little circle,
'I'm adopted,' without fearing your world's
gonna cave in, or that people are gonna
think bad of you all of a sudden. *(My legs feel*

kind of shaky. I put the dictionary back, sink
down on my bed.) "Once you say it to one
person, maybe it'll be easier to say it to
another. And down the road it'll seem
natural. It'll seem right to start writing those
letters, making those calls, doing what
you have to do to find your blood relatives.

"You'll even find the right words to talk
with your mom and dad about it. Really.
Just take one step at a time, Lizzie. Remember,
the first step toward searching is being able
to say the truth about who you are, without
feeling bad about it. One step at a time, girlie."
Okay. I can do that. One step, one word at a time.

WHAT I REMEMBER: SPRING

Catching pollywogs with Bob at Rothenburg's Pond, planting
carrots, peas, and lettuce with Gram, going to the canoe races
with Dad, how steam rose off the water early in the morning,
fishing for rainbows and sunnies with Bob at Fleming's Creek,
the smell of cut grass, lilacs, seeing the first robin

Mom in a chair under the crabapple tree, sketching its pink
                                        blossoms,
counting the school days left 'til summer vacation, getting
my appendix out when I was five (Mom thinking
the ice-cream man poisoned me)

Church on Easter Sunday, the priest in his purple
robes, coloring eggs, chocolate bunnies. Bob boasting that white
chocolate bunnies were the best, 'cause he was allergic to milk
chocolate... me always wondering where that came from—
was his birthmother or birthfather allergic, too?

AFTER PETER MEETS MY FAMILY

We're sitting on the picnic table, just
Peter and me, eating watermelon,
seeing who can spit the seeds the farthest

when he says out of the blue, "My brother
Sam doesn't look like anybody else in
our family. Just like you don't look like

anybody in yours. We always joke
around and tell him he's adopted. That
drives him nuts!" Peter laughs, looks at me like

I'm going to share this chuckle with him.
I spit a seed farther than ever, then
get up, my face red as watermelon,

and pretend to look for whatever bird
is chittering in the maple tree. "Hey,
Lizzie, what's wrong?" asks Peter, following

me. "Oh, nothing, nothing," I say. "Then why
are you crying?" he says, stepping closer.
"I'm not," I lie. "And hey, don't touch me."

SHARING SECRETS AT
JAMES BARD STATE PARK

"You tell me a secret
and I'll tell you one,"
Peter says, chewing
on a straw like some
kind of philosopher.
We're lying face-up
on a blanket
in the park, our
favorite place to talk.
I think, *No way*.
I wonder, *Do I really
trust him?*
I say, "You first."
He puts down
the straw and gets
up on one elbow
so he can look me
in the eye. "You
won't tell?" he asks.
With my left
forefinger I cross
my heart, then zip
my lips and throw
away the key. "Okay,
then," he whispers.
"I repeated first grade.
I'm really fifteen, turning
sixteen in three months."
My jaw nearly drops
but I catch it just
in time, and push up
on my elbow, too.
"Well, that doesn't
change how I feel,"
I say. Then I add,
"My brother repeated

second grade, and he's
the smartest person
I know." Peter smiles
(his almost-dimples
make me melt. They
could melt a rock). He
gives me a kiss. *"Thanks,"*
he says. "Now you."
"Oh—well, I, I,—"
I laugh nervously.
(Could I say it?
"One step at a time . . . ")
Peter takes my hand,
kisses me again.
A Frisbee lands
on our blanket.
Peter tosses it
back to a man
with dreadlocks
down to his waist.
Then says, "Come on,
Lizzie. Really."
"All right, all right,"
I say. "Remember
when we were in
third grade, that time
on the playground
when I punched
that girl
in the stomach?"
Peter grins. "From
what I heard,
she deserved it."
"That's right," I say.
"And, just between
you and me, I—

I kind of liked it."

THE BIRD

It must have been spring, after school or some
Saturday. Kate and I were out walking
in the woods near Fleming's Creek when one
of us stopped, then the other. A squeaking,
more like a cheeping from under a little fern
turned out to be a baby bird. Its eyes
were closed tight as if he hadn't learned
how to open them yet. We were surprised
he had no feathers, just fuzz the color of dirt.
"We have to save him!" I said, looking around
for something to carry him in. "He's hurt,"
said Kate. He'd stopped making any sound.
She meant he wouldn't live, and so I said a prayer
while Kate swore his mother would find him there.

MEETING THE FAMILY OF
PETER ROBERT WOODWARD IV

Peter Robert Woodward IV
looks so much like his father
Peter Robert Woodward III
who looked so much like
Peter Robert Woodward Jr.

who looked like the first
Peter Robert Woodward
that if you line up pictures
of all the Peter Roberts at age
ten, it's impossible to tell

one face from another face.
They all have nicknames, like
"Little Peter," and "Big Peter"
and "Grandpa Peter." My
Peter hates how his mom

lined up the photographs
almost as soon as I walked
in the door, so I could see
the family resemblances
for myself. He hates how

she always says, "Peter takes
after his father" and "Peter
comes from a long line
of meat & potato men"
and "Peter has his father's

brains and his grandfather's
way with a basketball." Peter's
little brother Sean looks
just like their mother, with
dark hair and that *long* neck.

Peter's sister looks just like
him, straight brown hair
and eyes so blue they make
you think you're in outer
space, looking back at Earth.

Peter's older brother Sam
doesn't take after anybody,
just like Peter said. He's
a hazel-eyed, guitar-playing
vegetarian with a long blond

ponytail. At dinner I'm psyched
to sit between Peter and Sam,
who looks so different, I feel
at home next to him. I think,
Wait 'till I tell Kate about *this!*

WHY NOT

Kate is stirring something yummy on the stove,
chili maybe, with chucks of something I can't
name. "Why don't you ask out Sam Woodward?"
I say, and Kate jumps like something just flew
out of the pot and bit her on the nose. "I mean,
why wait for him to ask you? Why not ask first?"
Kate relaxes her shoulders a little, starts stirring
again. "Oh, you wouldn't want to seem *that*
interested," she says. "Now, see how I added
tofu to the chili? No one will know it's not meat,"
she says. She spoons up some chili for me
to taste. "Yum! Great!" I say. "But why not? I mean,
why not ask out Sam?" I ask again. "You *know*,"
she says, "I mean—he's nice and all—but you
don't want to get yourself in a position where
you can get too attached. Besides, we're both
leaving for college soon. Going our separate
ways." "But, why? What's the harm in getting
attached?" I say. "Oh, you," she says. "*Silly.*"

WHEN I WAS LITTLE

When I was little I used to think
I'd better be good, I'd better
behave, or else Mom and Dad
might send me back.

When I was little, I used to think
I'd better get good grades,
I'd better do my chores, or else
Mom and Dad might send me back.

When I was little, I used to think
someday I'd get a letter, someday
I'd get a phone call from HER.
She'd say, I want you back.

When I was little, I used to think
she was like Mary Poppins,
and someday she'd come floating
back to me on her umbrella.

When I was little, I used to think
she'd better not come knocking
on our door, she'd better not think
I'd ever leave Mom & Dad.

When I was little, I used to think
Mom and Dad picked me out
like I was a new car. I prayed
I wouldn't be a lemon, that
they wouldn't turn me in
for a newer model.

I'M AMERICAN

How come people always like to talk about
their heritage and ask me when "my people"
came to America and where exactly my grand-
parents were born? How come people always
want to know if McLane is Irish or Scottish,
and if I'm one hundred percent Celtic, like they talk

about pedigrees of dogs? I mean, how nosy
can you get? And besides, I can't say the truth,
which is I don't even know if I'm really Irish
or Scottish, 'cuz then I'd have to say *why*
I don't know, and in my family we never talk
about THAT outside the four walls of our house

(except with Jan and Cath). So when Peter brought it
up the other day (his parents are so into being
English, they make jokes in fake British accents,
watch some weird TV show called "Fawlty Towers,"
and drink tea instead of coffee) I just said
"I'm American." Meaning, drop the subject!

DEBATING THE SECRETS

We're in Mr. Kingley's library, my favorite room
at Cathy's house (especially because I can borrow
whatever books I want) when I tell Cathy and Jan

how I'm starting to feel bad about keeping this huge
secret about myself from Peter. Jan, who's
sprawled across a chair like an open book, says

she doesn't tell many people she's adopted, either,
especially some boy who claims he likes you when
tomorrow he'll tell some other girl the same thing.

"Peter's not like that," I say. "So why haven't you
told him?" she says, and I take a book called *Leaves
of Grass* off a shelf and open it; read, "I celebrate myself,

and sing myself..."Cathy, who's taken over the other
comfortable chair, says, "Lizzie doesn't tell anybody.
It's her secret." She sits up straighter so she can look

right at Jan when she asks, "And who have you told
besides me and Lizzie? Oh, and Toshi?" Jan hesitates,
then answers, "Nobody...in school." I close the book.

I don't say I learned my lesson when we were little, when
those girls practically spit in Cathy's face, shouted
that crap about how her real mother didn't love her.

I don't say that I learned from watching my parents
and sister and brother what to say and what not to say
about being adopted. I don't say I feel sorry for Cathy;

she can't hide she's adopted, being half-black and half-
white with two white parents. And I don't remind Cathy
about the woman in the photograph she tells everyone

is her dead mother. Instead I say, "Can I borrow this
book?" Cathy shrugs and nods, so I slip *Leaves of Grass*
into my backpack. "Lots of people say it's no big deal

to be adopted. Like, so what," Jan says, making me
squirm. "They think, 'Oh, *everyone* knows someone who's adopted or gave up a baby for adoption or

had a baby and kept it and what's the *big deal*, today
we're all OPEN' (Jan throws her arms wide like she's
about to hug me, then lets them fall)...'We're all diverse

and ACCEPTING...' (*mmmHMM You go!* Cathy urges)
'and adoptees have nothing to be ashamed of, they're just
like everyone else.' I've got nothing to say to those people.

What can I say to somebody that ignorant?" This makes
me think, Well, maybe we can teach them something
about how we feel. Maybe we can start with our parents...

"You know, if *we* had had open adoptions, we'd know
from the start who our mother is," Cathy says. "There
wouldn't be so many secrets, and depending on what deal

she worked out, she could write us letters or call us
on the phone...maybe even visit on our birthdays!"
Jan says, "Don't count on it." "*Oh, Jan,*" Cathy cries,

"*I'm sorry! I forgot!*" Cathy sighs, sinking into her
chair as if she wants to disappear. "It's easy to forget,"
says Jan. "My birthmother read 'open' on my adoption

papers and thought it was a an open door for her to run
out and never look back." Jan pats the arm of her chair,
something my mom would do, inviting me to sit

down. "My parents would freak if my birthmother was
was able to call or visit," I say. "They'd worry I'd want
to be with her. It seems like even *wondering* about her means

I'm being disloyal." My voice is shaky. "Maybe we think
about this stuff too much," I whisper. "We *have to*—
nobody else does," says Jan. "What bugs me is how

some people say stupid stuff if you do tell them, like
how they always wished *they* were adopted, or how
taking you in was this 'generous thing' your parents

did, like we were some kind of charity cases. Like
we were homeless orphans who needed saving or
something." We all stop talking after Jan says that.

GIRL TALK

"Forget what I said. Don't tell Peter, don't ever tell
anyone you're adopted," Cathy warns one night

on the phone. I say, "But why? I thought you said—
what's going on? Why are you saying that?" "Because

then he'll think you're a reject," she blurts. This is how
I know Cathy and Max just broke up.

I can hear her crying. "Cath, you're not a reject,"
I say. "*Oh, Cath.* You're not. You're not."

KIND OF SAVIORS

"Think about it. Where would our parents be
if it weren't for us?" I say to Cathy, who's stretched
out on my bed. I'm on Kate's bed, trying to cheer
Cathy up. "They'd probably be on vacation,"
she says. (It's been two days since "it" happened:

Max called and said their long-distance "thing"
was too hard; then they had an ugly fight. Cathy
was so hurt! She said she felt like a reject—like
she was a reject since she was born.) "*My* parents?
They'd be in Bermuda. Or Florida." "No, really!" I say.

"Look, Cath, this room would be empty if my parents
weren't lucky enough to get me and Kate.
Bob's room would be empty—clean, but empty.
Boring! There'd be nobody at dinner but the two
of them. Boring. There'd be no one to yell at

but each other. Boring! There'd be no one to tell
them that their music is way old, no one to tell
them that they dress funny." (Cathy smiles at that.)
"They'd have no one to tell all those stories to
about when they were kids. The house would be

empty, except for them! They'd have no one
to take out the garbage or dust the living room!
They'd be clueless! They'd be lonely! *Bored!*
And doing all that housework!" "Okay, okay,"
Cathy says, cracking up. "So we actually *saved*

our parents," she says. "We're kind of saviors!
They should be thankful. They should look at us
every day and say, 'Thank goodness your own
mother didn't want you.'" Even that makes us
laugh, even though it also makes us want to cry.

THE BROKEN PLACE III

Sometimes the monster in that cave
just pulls me in and disappears
without a word. That's worse, when
he doesn't speak to me at all. It makes
me feel even more alone. I can see
everyone walking by: Mom and Dad,
Kate and Bob, sometimes even my
friends, but no one knows I'm here.
I try to call to them, but no one hears
what I'm saying. That's when I start
writing. I know it's the only way out.

CURE FOR THE BLUES

Sometimes the only sure cure for my blues
is reading poems. The best is reading

poems to other people, though mostly
I read them alone, out loud in my room

when Kate's not there. Mostly my friends think it's
kind of cool that I like poetry, but

most think I'm kind of nuts, too. They just don't
get it, they say. But sometimes we'll be at

a slumber party and it'll be real
late and Toshi or Jan will say, "Read us

something, Lizzie." They know I have a book
in my backpack. So I'll read them Lucille

Clifton's "Hips" or Hayden Carruth's "Cows at
Night" or Donald Hall's "Names of Horses" or

Anne Sexton's twisted fairy tale poems
or that Gwendolyn Brooks' poem

about the pool players or Cornelius
Eady's "Victims of the Latest Dance Craze"

and sometimes they say "Oh! *That's* poetry?"
But the best is when they say "Hey, Lizzie,

read us another one." And then my blues?
They pack their bags. They go on vacation.

LATE SPRING CLEANING

Dad is shoveling ashes and bits of burned wood
out of the living room fireplace while I hold
the bucket for him at an angle. "Helps keep

the dust down to a minimum," he says, which
is important to me, since it's my job to dust
the living room every Saturday. He looks tired

today, I think. A little pale. I worry that he works
too hard. I worry about his heart, which he says
is stronger than ever, since they put the new

valve in. That was four years ago, when I was
ten. "Your mother is worried about you,"
he says. "She says you've been awfully quiet,

spending more time than usual in your room."
Well, I think, everybody is worried about
everybody else. "I've been writing a lot, I say.

And reading." "Well, nothing wrong with that,"
Dad says. "Anything special you're working on?"
"*Yes,*" I say too quickly, then regret it. He stops

shoveling to look at me, really wanting to know.
"I've been writing about... you know. Stuff,"
I say, knowing how lame that sounds. "Well,"

he says, "anytime you want to share some,
I'm game. Remember, I'm Lizzie McLane's
biggest fan. Your mother is, too, you know—

she just worries a lot." My face feels so hot,
I'd swear there's still flames in that fireplace.
"Oh, *thanks,* Dad," I say. (How I'd love to show

him some poems! But, do I have the guts?
Do I dare?) "And," he says (he clears his
throat, which sounds kind of like a motorcycle

starting up) "whatever the poems are about—
your birthparents, or whatever—is just fine
with me." That's when I drop the bucket. Ashes

fly everywhere, on the rug, in my hair, on Dad's
jeans. Everything looks so bright all of a sudden:
his laughing face, my hands, the dirty fireplace.

I'm laughing, too, and already wondering which
poem I'll show him first. Maybe I'll *read* it to him.
Something inside me bursts like fireworks.

LIFE LESSONS

I.

It's a Saturday in early June.
Peter and I are at James Bard
State Park, lying on our
blanket. I'm not reading
him poems from a book.
We're not talking, we're just
holding hands, staring
at clouds. We don't have
lots to say because
we just got back from
a memorial service for
8 kids from Stone
Falls, the town next
to ours. All 8 kids
were 14, 15, 16—like us—
we didn't really know
them, but played against
some of them in basketball—
5 girls and 3 boys. One
was April—April, the only
girl as tall as me on the Stone
Falls team, April, number 5,
who smiled at me after that
game we almost won. April.
I knew her name.

Last week she and these
other kids skipped out
of school after lunch, went
down to Sammy Lake with
a case of beer and were
killed coming back on
Route 22. They hit a tree
and all of them are dead.

Just like that. April
is gone. She smiled at me.
She was tall and nice,
a good ball player and
she's gone. Just like that.

Peter is friends with a girl
from Stone Falls named
Jenny, who was part
of that group. She told him
last night on the phone
how she'd actually
gotten in the car
with those kids after lunch,
then realized she'd
forgotten her house keys
and had to go back
to her locker,
how she told them
to go ahead and have
fun before they got
caught skipping,
and how she waved
as they pulled out
of the parking lot.
Then, he said, she started
crying, and he couldn't
think of anything
to say that sounded
right, so he just let her
cry on the phone like that.

When I saw Peter
with his parents
at the Memorial Service,
we just hugged. Most
people were crying
and hugging, and we

felt kind of strange
because we didn't know
most of the people there.
Dad knew just about
everyone. He cried,
too. Later he offered
Peter a ride home with us.

Then Peter and I walked
here to the park,
like it was automatic,
as if it were any normal
day. So now I start
writing in my notebook,
thinking how fragile
everything is, how one minute
we're here and the next
we're not. I think, If
I never tell anyone
outside Cathy and Jan
my secret, I might die
without most people
knowing who I really am.

II.

I'm lying in bed with my
notebook again, thinking
for the zillionth time about
those 8 kids, about April,
picturing her getting into
that car. Then I have to stop
myself from thinking too
much about what happened
next. At the memorial

service, the priest said
they are all in heaven
now, with God. Said
they were happy. That
was supposed to make us
feel better, but really
it didn't. I mean, they
didn't even have a chance
to finish high school,
become artists or bee-
keepers or astronauts.
April might have gone
to college on a basketball
scholarship. Which makes
me think life's not fair—
makes me suck in my
breath to think how quick
it can end. Everything
you were can be gone,
just like that.

It might be time
to tell Peter everything
I am—the whole truth
about me. But I hear
the monster shuffling
around in my closet,
muttering. *That's bull.*
What a cliché! he huffs,
then mimics my thoughts,
'Oh, life is short, so
I'd better tell Peter my secret!'
"It's not bull," I say,
"You're wrong." He
snorts, *It belongs*
on a Hallmark card.
I take a deep breath,
feel something rising in me

like a river in a storm.
"A Hallmark card.
You're absolutely
right," I say
to the monster,
"You're *so* right,
I'm going to send *you*
that card before it's too late,
and sign it with x's
and o's, Love, Lizzie."
The monster shuts up.

Wow, do I feel better!
I fall asleep, dream
that I'm flying.

THE KEY

Saturday again, and Peter and I are at the park
(where else?) staring up into trees. My heart's
a little hummingbird inside my chest—I've decided
to tell Peter my secret—I'm shaking at first but
the words start to come. I tell him all about me, about
Kate, and Bob, and the phone call stories and
how I don't know what nationality I am or why
my mother couldn't keep me or what time
of day I was born. And know what Peter does?
He hugs me and says, "Thanks." He says, "Lizzie,
you're beautiful." Then with his right forefinger
he crosses my heart and then crosses his. He
crosses his finger over his lips, locks my secret
inside him, and throws away the pretend key.
But I pick up that key and put it in my pocket.
I think I'm going to need it someday soon, when
I'm really ready to let that secret out.

GOOD STUDENT

(Poem I left on Mom's easel today)

I study women's faces, women's bodies.
I study chins, knees, necks. I'm looking
for a beauty mark shaped like Florida, for
brown eyes ringed by blue. I'd like
to say hello to a woman and hear my own
voice echo back, *Hello, nice to meet you.*
The woman I'm looking for might be left-
handed. Freckles might shower her arms,
her cheeks. Her right ear might feature
a little bump, a peak. I study women's faces,
women's bodies, in church, on the street,
at the grocery store. I'm a good student.
Not many escape my gaze. If they gave out
grades in "resemblance searching," I'd get
an A. I check out skinny women, fat women,
short women—though tall ones interest me
more. At the zoo, at the beach, at the mall,
I'm not looking for a mother—I already have
a great one, you see. I'm just hoping to meet
a woman, *the* woman who looks like me.

SUMMER JOB BLUES

There's no job for me at the mall until I'm sixteen
Can't do much at all until I turn sixteen
. . . mall's too crowded anyway, people packed in like Sue in her
                                                    tight jeans

I could lifeguard at the Y where a kid bit me last summer
I was life guarding at the Y and this kid bit me last summer
Maybe I'll call the Y, though just the thought's a total bummer

There might be work selling strawberries at Red Oak's Mill Farm
Maybe I could pick what's in season at Red Oak's Mill Farm
I could spend all day outside, come home smelling like a barn

Of course I'll be babysitting Samaya and Joah down the street
I love babysitting Samaya and Joah Pulido down the street
Though I'll gain weight for *sure*—their fridge is full of snacks
                                                    and treats

I wish someone would pay me just to lie in the sun
I'd read books and take naps, just lying in the sun
and tell my parents I found a job studying "effects of
                                                    illumination"!

WIDENING THE CIRCLE

We are The Bloodhounds, The Secret
Smashers, the Foundlings who found
each other. We three—Cathy, Jan,
and me—formed a circle inside
our circle of friends and named it
"private." Now we figure it's time
to stop being so scared, time to make
space for Toshi, Deb, and Barb, who
are sitting with us in a circle
on the floor of my room. Inside the ring
of us are three candles. Cathy lights
the first one, then pulls the framed
photograph out of her backpack.
"This isn't really my birthmother,"
she begins, and tells the story of her
nutty birthparents, the ones she found
but kept secret from everyone but Jan
and me. Then Jan lights the next candle—
"Only Cathy, Lizzie, and Toshi know
this," she begins, and tells how
she was born at the Home for Little
Wanderers, how she was adopted
when she was two days old, how
she didn't like to talk about it
because she was afraid she must
have been a bad baby somehow,
if her own mother didn't want her.
Then I light the third candle
and begin, "In my house, there's no
such thing as stories about when
we were born. In my house, we have
what we call 'the Phone Call Stories'..."
and when I'm talking, Toshi takes
my right hand and Jan takes my left,
and then we're all holding hands.

We are a circle. My friends almost look
like angels in the candlelight. I think,
This is what it means to be sisters.

TWO OF ME

Sometimes I feel like two different people.
One of me felt lit up like a candle
after I told Barb and Deb and Toshi
that I'm adopted—it was as if

they were meeting me for the first
time, and they really really liked me.
That night I think I took the deepest breath
ever. I could have floated away. But

the next day, this other me took over,
and I felt like I'd lost something. I had
the same feeling the day after I told Peter.
Isn't that crazy? I mean, I thought being

open, *saying* "I'm adopted," at least
to my closest friends, would make the idea
of telling people easier. But instead this
other me feels like...there was something

I've been holding onto all my life, something
that has a lot of power, like a magic stone
in my pocket. And now—well, I've got
the stone in my hands; I'm letting people

see it. I'm holding it out instead of in,
and I might drop it. It might fall right out
of my hands. Somebody might take it. (Who?
Nobody, the other me says.) It's not the same

stone anymore. I can't put it back in my pocket
and pretend I never brought it out. (Isn't that
what I wanted, to bring it out? But it's scary.
Confusing!) Would anybody ever understand

what this other me is trying to say? Cathy would
tell me, "No matter what, every morning look
in the mirror and say, 'You're doin' great!
You go, girlie!'" Thinking about that makes me

smile, and flip back to being the other me
again, feeling proud and glad, 'cause it *was*
a big deal, a huge step I took when I said
those words. I *said* them, and didn't even cry.

NOTES FOR A LETTER
I MIGHT WRITE SOMEDAY

Dear New York Foundling,

My name is Elizabeth Ann McLane
My adopted name is Elizabeth Ann McLane
My name is Elizabeth—I was named that twice

I was told you could tell me
I was wondering if you could tell me
I was hoping you could help me

I am the daughter of Margaret and Patrick McLane
I am the daughter of a woman you once knew
I am two daughters

Would you please tell me everything you know about me
Could you tell me what my records say about me
I was told I had the right to know about my birthmother

I'd like to know what you can tell me about my birthmother,
                                                    my birth
please send everything the law says you're allowed to tell me
please send what they call "non-identifying information"

I know you can't tell me where my mother is
You can't tell me my mother's name
You can't tell me if she'd know me if she saw me on the street

But I'd like her to know I have the best family ever
I have the best family anyone could ever have
I want her to know I love my mom and dad, my sister and
                                                    brother

I know you can't tell me much but ... I just want to know why
                                                 she gave me up
I want to know if she ever thinks of me
I want her to know I'm happy

I want to know if she likes (writes?) poetry
... Am I really Irish *or not?*
I want to know if she thinks I was a mistake

Did she ever tell you who my birthfather is?
Are you allowed to tell me stuff about my birthfather, too?
I'm not ready to think much about my birthfather—yet

You probably can't answer most of my questions
I know you probably can only tell me a few facts
I know you have lots in my file I'm not supposed to see

But there's things I want to know
There's things I have a right to know
It's my birthright to know

There's some things I need to say to my birthmother
Can you send a note for me to my birthmother?
Will I ever have a chance to talk with her?

I want her to know she did the right thing
I want her to know ... I don't need her to be my mother
I want to be friends ... I want to say thanks

IN MY ROOM, I READ DAD A POEM

If Mom is a window, Dad is
a door, a sturdy screen
door that lets the breezes
in and keeps the bugs
out. The door is usually not
locked. When I read Dad my poem
"A Matter of Loyalty," I see
that door start to swing out
toward me. When I get to the last
line, Dad throws the door open
and I step into the room
that his arms make. That's when
I see Mom, who's been listening
from the hallway. She comes in,
puts her arms around Dad and me,
and together we make a house.

Afterword

When I was writing the poems in this book, it felt as if someone was whispering them into my ear. When people ask me where the poems came from, what inspired them, I say they were written by the fourteen-year-old girl I wish I'd been. There wasn't anything magical or supernatural going on; I wasn't really channeling the words of a girl named Lizzie McLane. But many authors say that the characters in their stories show up like unexpected guests at all hours, and it's the author's job to write down what those characters say and do. That's what it felt like for me: Lizzie walked into the room where I write and started dictating poems, and I started listening, started writing them down.

One of the first questions people ask me when they read my poems is: *Did this really happen? Are these poems based on your life?* The truth is yes, and no. Some of the things that happen in this book really did happen in my own life, although many of them did not. Many of the characters are based on real people, or combinations of people, while some of them are completely imaginary. In any case, which events are actual events and which characters are inspired by "real" people doesn't matter, because all of the *emotions* expressed in the poems are true. I had to write the poems because there was no other way to say what I meant and felt. That's what poetry can do: it tries to express what seems impossible to say otherwise. Meaning, if I could have *told* someone how I felt, I wouldn't have had to write poems about it. Poems are often how I communicate.

Like Lizzie, I was adopted. My older sister and brother were adopted, too. We grew up in a place a lot like New Hook, in New York State's Hudson Valley. The Hudson River was just a few miles away, and there were woods, dairy farms, and apple orchards close by. New York City was a two-hour train ride south of us. Like Lizzie, Kate, and Bob, my older sister and brother and I were born there.

I feel as though I always knew I was adopted. Maybe that's because I was the third adopted child in my family; adoption was part of our family culture. Our parents were loving, supportive people who made it clear that we were their children even though we weren't their flesh and blood. Mom and Dad were strict, but they were also affectionate and caring. They told us often that they were proud of us. My sister and brother and I knew we were loved.

Mom was a terrific cook and Dad was a great storyteller, so dinner was a favorite time of day for all of us when I was a kid. Dinner was when we did most of our talking, catching up on school sports

(I played basketball and softball, swam on our church's youth team, and rowed crew for a couple of years) and what was going on at school in general. School talk was a huge thing in our house because my father was a principal—in fact, he was *my* principal from kindergarten through sixth grade. Some of the things my father spoke about, private things about students and teachers I knew, were not meant to be repeated. He and my mother reminded us often that "What's said in this house does not leave this house." We kids respected that, realizing we were privileged to be included so often in my parents' conversations about my father's work.

This rule about keeping what's said in the house confidential grew out of the need to respect and protect the privacy of people in our community, though it spilled over into family matters, too. We learned to be private people in many ways, and not indulge in gossip. This carried over into how we spoke about adoption. The fact that my sister and brother and I were adopted was a secret we kept from the world. Relatives and a sprinkling of my parents' friends were the only people who knew, and the subject was never discussed even in their company, at least in front of us kids. The reason for this was never discussed, either, though it probably had to do with my parents' heart-felt insistence that we were like any other family. Their children were their children, period, end of subject. But in my heart I carried the awful "truth": that my parents loved me *despite* the fact that I was not their flesh and blood, *despite* the fact that I was damaged goods. So I thought. My parents were protecting me from the shame of being an adoptee. So I thought. Not speaking of being adopted thus became my way of life as well. That as few people knew as possible seemed vital to my emotional and social survival.

So, although we occasionally spoke about adoption at home, there were unspoken limits around what could be said. How I came to understand what was all right to say and ask and what was taboo was part instinct, part trial and error. The scene in Lizzie's poem "Reading My Poem 'What I Want' to Mom" comes close to describing something that happened to me when I was in sixth grade. I'd written a poem about my birthmother—the first one I ever wrote about her, I think—wondering who she was and whether she ever thought about me. When I read my mom this poem, she had the same reaction as Lizzie's mom. She might have mumbled something like "That's very nice, dear," but basically she turned pale and ran out of my bedroom.

This was how I learned that it was all right for my sister and brother and me to talk about the facts of our adoption, but not our feelings. For the most part, we felt happy, lucky, and grateful for our parents and each other. That's what we were supposed to feel. But if we also felt sad or confused sometimes about being adopted, those feelings were to be kept to ourselves. It was okay to ask questions, as long as they didn't give the impression that we'd rather be anyplace other than where we were. And because that was true—I didn't want any other family than the one I had—I stuck to this unspoken rule.

Our parents freely and joyously shared all the details they could remember about how my sister and brother and I "arrived." These stories were mainly about what my parents were doing when the New York Foundling Hospital in Manhattan called with the good news that we were available for adoption. I loved these family anecdotes, and asked to hear them again and again. They are very similar to "The Phone Call Stories" that Lizzie writes about.

I think I always asked more questions than my brother or sister did about other adoption-related facts, too. (My brother and sister probably wondered about this stuff just as much, but they didn't come right out and ask about it as often as I did.) Because the three of us were adopted from the New York Foundling, which is a Roman Catholic agency, there was a very good chance that all of our birthmothers were Catholic. (Birthfathers were even more of a mystery in every way.) The Foundling provided a few more sketchy details about each of us, although none of it ever seemed certain. I wanted to know more. For instance, what nationality was I? Mom and Dad said they *thought* I was Austrian and Irish (with Mom being German and Dad being Irish, this made for a near-perfect match), but they weren't sure.

This made me crazy, not really knowing where my ancestors, my blood relatives, were from. What I wanted to know most, though, was who my birthmother was and why she gave me away. I was not hoping to be "rescued" from my parents. I felt fiercely loyal to my family and did not wish to go live with my "real mother" or anyone else. But I was divided, wanting my mom and dad to know that I loved them as much as they loved me, but also longing to know who my birthmother was, wanting to meet someone who looked like me. At the same time, I lived in fear of what, as a girl, I called "the broken place." The broken place, which haunts Lizzie, too, is where my truth lurked like a terrible secret always about to expose itself to the world. This was the unspeakable flaw I was born with: my mother had abandoned me because I was a mistake from the moment of my accidental conception. She was not supposed to get pregnant. I was unwanted and unlovable. This is what I told myself when I was feeling down.

My parents never gave me reason to feel this way. They didn't know about "the broken place"; if they had known, I'm sure they would have tried to help me escape it once and for all. But in order to do that, we would have had to talk more openly than we ever did before. It would have had to have been okay for me to say how often I wondered about my birthmother, and how it made me sad sometimes to think I might never know her. It would have had to have been okay for me to say that someday I might look for her. It would have had to have been okay for me to search for answers to questions my parents could never answer themselves.

But it was not okay. If I had said and asked these things, I feared it would have made my parents think they weren't doing a good job, that I wanted my "real" parents. They would have felt as if they'd failed me somehow, that I didn't love them as much as they loved me. Of course I never wanted my parents to feel this way, never wanted to hurt them. I was an adult by the time I realized that wanting to know where I came from had nothing to do with my feelings for Mom and Dad; that it is not a sign of disloyalty to ask hard questions. But it did seem that way to all of us—to me, to my sister and brother, to my parents—when I was young.

According to the Evan B. Donaldson Adoption Institute,* there are about 1.5 million adopted children in the United States today. And more than sixty percent of Americans know someone who is adopted, someone who has given up a child for adoption, or someone who has adopted children. And there were more than 250,000 international adoptions (adoptions of children from other countries by United States citizens) between 1971 and 2001, and these have more than doubled since 1990. More than sixty percent of these children have been girls. International adoptions are usually arranged through adoption agencies. Depending on the laws of the country where the child lives, the adoptions are finalized either abroad or in the United States.

While many people today talk more openly about being adopted or having adopted children, they still face many of the issues and problems that my family and I did. Until the late 1970s, most adoptions were "closed." This meant that once a mother signed the papers to give up her baby for adoption, she and her child would probably never see each other again. Because the adoption was closed, the birthmother would never know who had adopted her baby or have any contact with the child. Likewise, the adoptive parents would be

*www.adoptioninstitute.org

given few details about the child's background and would not know the birthmother's name, or the child's. The child would never know who his (or her) mother was or where she was from, why she gave him up, or who his father was. He would not know much about his own medical history, either—if, for instance, cancer or high blood pressure or heart disease ran in his blood family.

Lizzie's adoption was closed, as was Kate's, Bob's, and mine. My adoption records are sealed and filed somewhere in Albany, New York, along with my birth certificate. When I was adopted, a new birth certificate was produced with my new name on it. Adoptees are the only U.S. citizens without the right to see or own their original birth certificates. According to Adam Pertman's book *Adoption Nation* (Basic Books, 2000), Alaska and Kansas are the only two states that have always kept adoption and birth records open. Only three other states offer adoptees unrestricted access to their adoption records and original birth certificates: Alabama, New Hampshire, and Oregon; these states opened their records between 1998 and 2005. Delaware and Tennessee allow access to birth records, but with restrictions. (Cathy was born in Michigan, where access rules are also less restrictive and adoptive parents have been known to help their adopted teens search for their birth parents.)

Originally, closed adoptions were supposed to protect the adults involved: the birthmother, who was probably not married when she had the baby, which years ago made her shameful in the eyes of society; and the adoptive parents, who would never have to worry about the birthmother changing her mind and coming back into her child's life in any way. The people making these decisions about closed adoptions assumed that this was all in "the best interest of the child," too. They thought kids like Lizzie and me were better off forgetting we had ever had another mother, better off bonding only with our adoptive parents. It was supposed to be less confusing for us that way.

Even though things are changing, many new adoptions today are still closed. Some adoptive parents just feel more secure knowing there will be no contact with their baby's birthmother. Some birthmothers find comfort in this, too. While Cathy's adoption was closed, her birthmother was able to handpick her adoptive parents. This is fairly common today. If an adoption can't be open, I think that allowing birthmothers (and sometimes birthfathers) a voice in who adopts their children is a positive trend.

"Open" adoptions, as opposed to "closed" ones, started becoming fairly common in the early 1980s. Open adoptions give birth and adoptive families some kind of contact with each other, but just how much varies quite a lot. Jan's adoption was open, so her birthmother had more than just a say in who adopted her. When the adoption took place, Jan's new parents were able to make an agreement with her birthmother about how much contact they would have with each other. Jan knows her birthmother's name, address, and medical history. (Jan's birthmother probably would have provided any information she knew about Jan's birthfather's medical history, too.)

Jan's birthmother also has Jan's address and phone number. If she wants to, she can call, send and receive photographs and letters, or even visit Jan. But in some open adoptions, like Jan's, there's just an exchange of information and photographs when the baby is born, and that's it. In other cases—and this is something that's starting to happen more and more—the birthmother (and even other blood relatives) call or write frequently, visit occasionally, and even spend some holidays with their child's adoptive family. Many babies and youngsters today are also being adopted by family members and friends—people who already have a connection to the birthmother's family. These tend to be the most open adoptions of all.

The less secretive people are about adoption, the better, I think. As Lizzie and I both know, secrets can be poisonous. What I had to learn (as Lizzie is coming to learn in this book) is that there is nothing to be ashamed of just because I'm adopted. What Lizzie's and my parents had to learn is that we adoptees have a right to know who we are and where we came from, and this has nothing to do with how much we love our moms and dads or what great parents they are. All of us had to learn that by talking and expressing how we feel, we understand each other better. Our bond grows stronger.

Although I believe that all adopted people have a right to their birth records, I think that if an adoptee wants to search for her or his birth parents, it's healthiest for all concerned if he or she is at least eighteen years old. Searching is not something an adoptee should decide to do on a whim, or without a lot of soul-searching. There are so many "unknowns" involved, so many things that can come up emotionally and factually—I think it takes the mind and heart of an adult who's done as much preparation as possible (reading, participating in adoption support groups, talking with family) to handle what it takes to search.

That said, people who were adopted in the United States who are interested in searching for their birth parents should start the process by contacting the agency that handled their adoption and asking for what's called "non-identifying information." This information will include everything the agency knows about an adoptee's birth parents and circumstances of his or her birth, without identifying who the parents are or where they live. People who were adopted privately—through a lawyer, for example—might have a more difficult time, but should start by contacting the law firm, if possible. People who were adopted outside the United States face even more challenges than people who were adopted domestically, but there are organizations and other resources that can help. The International Soundex Reunion Registry (ISRR) is a nonprofit group with a good reputation, and any adoptee (or birthparent) can use its services for free. It is a "mutual consent" registry, which means that both an adoptee and a birth relative must sign up separately, basically saying she/he wants to be found; then if there is a "match" of information, the ISRR helps them contact each other. There is a list of books that should prove useful to all adoptees interested in this topic at the end of *The Secret of Me*.

Every family has secrets. Lizzie and her friends talk about this in "Crossing Our Hearts in the Dark." I've heard people say that having a poet in the family is a curse, because we write about things the family seldom talks about, especially with outsiders. While some facts or stories do need to be kept private (usually to protect someone from getting hurt), for the most part I think it's healthy to talk about the things that happen to us and how we feel about them. Sometimes I understand something (an experience, an event, something someone said) in my head, but it's not until I write about it that I start to understand it in my heart.

A poet named Jack Gilbert says "poetry is a way to eat your life." In other words, by writing about an experience—hearing the words in your head, tasting them in your mouth, digesting them, putting them on paper—you can start to understand what they mean and how you feel about them. Some people never take the time to stop and think about their lives—not just think, but *feel*. That's what poems are for. They make us slow down. They help us make sense of our world.

Writing and reading helps Lizzie sort out her feelings about lots of things: her relationship with Kate and Bob, her parents, her friends, and Peter; her lack of self-confidence about her looks; and what it means to be adopted. Poetry—reading and writing it—has helped me sort out these kinds of issues since I was in elementary school. I know Lizzie would agree when I say that I hope other people will discover the power of poetry, too.

Guide to This Book's Poetics

Throughout this book, Lizzie writes a mix of formal poems and what's known as "free verse." The following is a brief guide for teachers and students of poetry who might be interested in taking a closer look at some of the forms and devices Lizzie employs.

End-stopped lines vs. Enjambed lines: Lines that have a logical pause at their close (usually with a period at the line's end) are "end-stopped;" lines are "enjambed" when the sense of one line runs over into the succeeding line. Both types of lines are found throughout the book.

Here is an example of an enjambed line from "When I Was Little":

> I'd better do my chores, or else
> Mom and Dad might send me back.

The first line could stand on its own grammatically; it makes sense as a sentence in which "or else" could seem almost threatening. The meaning of "or else" is extended by the next, enjambed line, where the reader learns the answer to "or else *what?*" ("Mom and Dad might send me back.")

Here is an example of two end-stopped lines from "Kind of Saviors":

> she was a reject since she was born.) "My parents?
> They'd be in Bermuda. Or Florida." "No, really!" I say.

Each line makes its own kind of sense, and ends with punctuation.

And here is a couplet from "How I Arrived" that exemplifies an enjambed line followed by an end-stopped line:

> a name. I had teeth. My legs bowed like a wish-
> bone. I could stretch my knees behind my head.

"My legs bowed like a wish" could stand on its own—it make its own strange sense—but with the next line the meaning is completed: the reader comes to understand her legs bow like a "wishbone." The rest of line two is a complete sentence, stopped at its end by a period.

Blues poems: "Cure for the Blues," "Summer Job Blues"

While many formal poetic forms come to us from Europe and Asia, blues poems are American through and through. They are inspired by the musical form known as "the blues," which spring from African musical roots. Blues poems are usually written in a first-person voice. The "classic" blues form is rhymed tercets, or three-line stanzas with rhyming end words, in which the first line makes a statement that is *repeated* with a twist or alteration in the second line. The third line then goes on to make an ironic contrast or extension of what's been said in the first two lines.

The writer Ralph Ellison said the blues "at once express the agony of life and the possibility of conquering it through sheer toughness of spirit." These poems usually talk about suffering, struggle, and the heartbreak side of romance. They take on life without flinching, often with wit, sarcasm, and humor. All blues poems don't have to follow the traditional form; some are just plain blue in what they have to say.

Free verse: Some people think that "free verse" means the poet doesn't have to follow any rules, and can create a poem that has no structure. Actually, there's nothing free about free verse. When a poet writes in free verse, the poem begins to impose its own rules, its own structure upon itself. Once the poet sees what that structure is, it's up to him or her to follow it. For example, if the lines of a free-verse poem start organizing themselves in couplets, and in lines that are of medium length (say about 10 or 11 syllables), the poet will probably want to create the entire poem in couplets with medium-length lines.

"Life Lessons" is an example of a poem written in free verse. Although there is no established stanza length (set number of lines per stanza), all of the lines are fairly short (ranging from six to nine syllables on average). This is because the first few lines of the poem were originally written this way, and felt "right" for the emotion of the piece; it then seemed right to continue with this line length throughout the poem. Also, in this poem all of the numbers are written as digits instead of being written out; this was also part of the poem's style that began early on and so was continued throughout.

Some of the many free-verse poems in the book include "Family Portrait," "The Wave," "Cathy's Story," "Why Not," and the seasonal sequence of the "What I Remember" poems.

List poem: "What I Want," "Adopt a Useless Blob," "When I was Little"

Also called a "catalog poem," this form has been around for a long time. (The *Bible*'s "Book of Genesis," for example, can be considered a list poem that traces the lineage of Adam and Eve's children.) List poems, which basically itemize things or events, can be made of lines of any length, rhymed or unrhymed.

Pantoum: "Crazy Love Pantoum"

This is a French form similar to the villanelle. The second and fourth lines of each quatrain repeat as the first and third in the next, and so on. Though the number of possible quatrains is indefinite, the second and fourth lines of the final stanza must repeat the first and third lines of the first stanza. Notice how circular this form is, with the first line also being the last line.

Rhyme: There are various approaches to rhyme throughout the book; here are just some examples. [Note: While not essential to a poem, rhyme accentuates a poems' *rhythm*. And as all poets know, *you gotta have rhythm...*]

END-RHYME: repetition of sound(s) are found at the end of lines (as in the sonnets, "Dumb," and "What to Wear to the Dance? I Worry and Kate Gives Advice")

NEAR-RHYME: sounds repeated are very close, but not exact: as in "e-Love" ("send" & "then," "date" & "ape"); "Crazy Love Pantoum" ("email" and "nails," "boring" and "fighting"); "Health Lesson" ("preach" and "disease")

INTERNAL RHYME: repetition of sounds within a line(s) and/ or stanza(s); just a few examples: "How I Arrived" ("five" "I" "ride" "cried"); "Self Portrait" ("rises" "surprise" and "too" "through"); "Two Mothers" ("mother" "other"); "Reading My Poem 'What I Want' to Mom" ("night" "tight," and "bed" "said") "Slumber Party" ("slugs" "rug" and "chair" "bear" fair")

ALLITERATION: repetition or echo of the first sound of several words in a line; "Dumb" would be an extreme example ("dumb dumb dumb"); also see "How I Arrived" (slow, sea-sick) and "What I Remember: Summer" ("sun," "soda, sunscreen," "sunburns")

IDENTICAL RHYME: the same word is repeated as rhyme (such as in "Dumb," "Different," and "What to Wear to the Dance? I Worry and Kate Gives Advice")

Sestina: "Searching Sestina"

A form that consists of six stanzas of six lines each, with a concluding tercet. It is usually unrhymed, but the end words of the first stanza force a pattern on to the poem that's like a rhyme scheme, because they are all repeated in the succeeding stanzas in a strict order that varies with each stanza, and some repeat again in the tercet.

The repeating end words in "Searching Sestina" are: (1) stuck, (2) history, (3) dance, (4) dates, (5) going, and (6) waste (Lizzie plays with this last word by substituting "waist"). The order in which these words are written set up the pattern for the rest of the poem. The whole thing has to go like this:

```
1,2,3,4,5,6
6,1,5,2,4,3
3,6,4,1,2,5
5,3,2,6,1,4
4,5,1,3,6,2
2,4,6,5,3,1
5,3,1
```

The tercet at the end goes 5, 3,1, but if the poet is truly being strict (which Lizzie isn't), these last three lines must also include end words 2, 4, 6, either at the start or in the middle of the lines.

Sonnets: "e-love," "e-love Gone Bad," "The Bird"

A form most people are familiar with, the standard sonnet has 14 lines written in iambic pentameter. There are different kinds of sonnets, like "Italian" and "Shakespearean" forms, which have different rules about stanza breaks and rhyme schemes.

Lizzie's are really "sonnet-like" in that they follow the 14-line limit and rhyme scheme of sonnets, though are not in strict iambic pentameter. "The Bird," with its pentameter lines, comes the closest to being a "pure" sonnet in terms of both rhyme and meter.

"Strict" Stanzas: (lines of poetry organized so that they form a pattern, which is repeated throughout)

COUPLETS: (pairs of lines) "Reading My Poem...to Mom," "Jan Tells Her Story," "Dumb" (also has a rhyme scheme); "Friends," "History Lesson," "Wishing," "Cure for the Blues," "Girl Talk"

TERCETS: (lines grouped in 3s) "Two Mothers," "The Broken Place," "The Wave," "Parents' Night," "My New 'Best Friend,'" "Love Sick," "After Peter Meets My Family," "Debating the Secrets," "Late Spring Cleaning"

QUATRAINS: (lines grouped in 4s) "Self Portrait," "Another One of Us," "Crossing Our Hearts in the Dark," "Different" (also has an "identical rhyme" scheme), "Food Fight," "When I Was Little" (also has a repeating/identical" line scheme), "A Secret's Out at Dinner," and "Two of Me"

OTHERS: "Sense of Smell" (5-line stanzas), "Word Pictures of Kate & Bob" (6-line stanzas), "Slumber Party" (10-line stanzas), "Food Fight" (5-line stanzas), "Phone Call Stories" (11), "Taboo Subject" (7-line stanzas, +1), "Mistakes" (5 lines), "Dance" (11), "Meeting the Family of Peter Robert Woodward VI" (5), and "Cathy's Best Advice" (7); "I'm American" (6); "Kind of Saviors" (5)

Syllabic Verse: the determining feature is the number of syllables in a line: "Bad News, Good News" (8 syllables per line), "Cure for the Blues" (10 syllables per line, also organized in couplets)

Simile/metaphor: when unlike ideas/images, or unlikely resemblances are paired/yoked; similes are easy to spot because they use the words "like" or "as." The book is full of metaphors and similes—for example in "Reading My Poem... to Mom" ("her face was / an open window"); and in "Another One of Us," Ms. Hubbard "beams like a flashlight." The monster in "The Broken Place" sequence is also a metaphor for the feeling Lizzie has during those times when she doesn't feel good about herself.

Villanelle: "What Sisters Are For"
This form, like the sestina and pantoum, comes from the French. It is made of five tercets and a quatrain (19 lines total). The first and third lines of the first tercet take turns repeating at the end of the tercets that follow, and both lines repeat as the last two lines of the poem. Notice that there are only two rhymes in the poem, determined by the end words of the poem's first two lines.

Some Poems Lizzie Loves

The following are some of the poems Lizzie mentions in *The Secret of Me,* poems she has read over and over again because she loves them so much.

Hayden Carruth
THE COWS AT NIGHT

The moon was like a full cup tonight,
too heavy, and sank in the mist
soon after dark, leaving for light

faint stars and the silver leaves
of milkweed beside the road,
gleaming before my car.

Yet I like driving at night
in summer and in Vermont:
the brown road through the mist

of mountain-dark, among farms
so quiet, and the roadside willows
opening out where I saw

the cows. Always a shock
to remember them there, those
great breathings close in the dark.

I stopped, and took my flashlight
to the pasture fence. They turned
to me where they lay, sad

and beautiful faces in the dark,
and I counted them—forty
near and far in the pasture,

turning to me, sad and beautiful
like girls very long ago
who were innocent, and sad

because they were innocent,
and beautiful because they were
sad. I switched off my light.

But I did not want to go,
not yet, nor knew what to do
if I should stay, for how

in that great darkness could I explain
anything, anything at all.
I stood by the fence. And then

very gently it began to rain.

Lucille Clifton

HOMAGE TO MY HIPS

these hips are big hips
they need space to
move around in.
they don't fit into little
petty places. these hips
are free hips.
they don't like to be held back.
these hips have never been enslaved,
they go where they want to go
they do what they want to do.
these hips are mighty hips.
these hips are magic hips.
I have known them
to put a spell on a man and
spin him like a top!

Cornelius Eady

VICTIMS OF THE LATEST DANCE CRAZE

The streamers choking the main arteries
Of downtown.
The brass band led by a child
From the home for the handicapped.
The old men
Showing their hair (what's left of it),
The buttons of their shirts
Popping in time
To the salsa flooding out
Of their portable headphones,

And mothers letting their babies
Be held by strangers.
And the bus drivers
Taping over their fare boxes
And willing to give directions.

Is there any reason to mention
All the drinks are on the house?
Thick, adolescent boys
Dismantle their BB guns.
Here is the world (what's left of it),
In brilliant motion,
The oil slick at the curb
Danced into a thousand
Splintered steps.
The bag ladies toss off their
Garments
To reveal wings.

"This dance you do," drawls the cop,
"What do you call it?"
We call it scalding the air.
We call it dying with your
Shoes on.
And across the street
The bodies of tramps
Stumble
In a sober language.

And across the street
Shy young girls step behind
Their nameless boyfriends,
Twirling their skirts.

And under an archway
A delivery boy discovers
His body has learned to speak,
And what does this street look like
If not a runway,
A polished wood floor?

From the air,
Insects drawn by the sweat
Alight, when possible,
On the blur
Of torsos.
It is the ride
Of their tiny lives.

The wind that burns their wings,
The heaving, oblivious flesh,
Mountains stuffed with panic,
An ocean
That can't make up its mind.
They drop away
With the scorched taste
Of vertigo.

And under a swinging light bulb
Some children
Invent a game
With the shadow the bulb makes,
And the beat of their hearts.
They call it dust in the mouth.
They call it horse with no rider.
They call it school with empty books.

In the next room
Their mother throws her dress away to chance.
It drops to the floor
Like a brush sighs across a drum head,

And when she takes her lover,
What are they thinking of
If not a ballroom filled with mirrors,
A world where no one has the right
To stumble?

In a parking lot
An old man says this:
"I am a ghost dance.
I remember the way my hair felt,
Damp with sweat and wind.

When the wind kisses the leaves, I am dancing.
When the subway hits the third rail, I am dancing.
When the barrel goes over Niagara Falls, I am dancing.
Music rings my bones like metal.
O, Jazz has come from heaven," he says,
And at the z he jumps, arcing his back like a heron's neck,
And stands suddenly revealed
As a balance demon,
A home for
Stetson hats.

We have all caught the itch:
The neon artist
Wiring up his legs,
The tourist couple
Recording the twist on their
Instamatic camera,
And in a factory,
A janitor asks his broom
For a waltz,
And he grasps it like a woman
He'd have to live another
Life to meet,
And he spins around the dust bin
And machines and thinks:
Is everybody happy?
And he spins out the side door,
Avoiding the cracks in the sidewalk,
Grinning as if he'd just received
The deepest kiss in the world.

Donald Hall

NAMES OF HORSES

All winter your brute shoulders strained against collars, padding
and steerhide over the ash hames, to haul
sledges of cordwood for drying through spring and summer,
for the Glenwood stove next winter, and for the simmering range.

In April you pulled cartloads of manure to spread on the fields,
dark manure of Holsteins, and knobs of your own clustered with oats.
All summer you mowed the grass in meadow and hayfield, the
mowing machine
clacketing beside you, while the sun walked high in the morning;

and after noon's heat, you pulled a clawed rake through the same acres,
gathering stacks, and dragged the wagon from stack to stack,
and the built hayrack back, uphill to the chaffy barn,
three loads of hay a day from standing grass in the morning.

Sundays you trotted the two miles to church with the light load
of a leather quartertop buggy, and grazed in the sound of hymns.
Generation on generation, your neck rubbed the windowsill
of the stall, smoothing the wood as the sea smooths glass.

When you were old and lame, when your shoulders hurt bending
to graze,
one October the man, who fed you and kept you, and harnessed
you every morning,
led you through corn stubble to sandy ground above Eagle Pond,
and dug a hole beside you where you stood shuddering in your skin,

and lay the shotgun's muzzle in the boneless hollow behind your ear,
and fired the slug into your brain, and felled you into your grave,
shoveling sand to cover you, setting goldenrod upright above you,
where by next summer a dent in the ground made your monument.

For a hundred and fifty years, in the pasture of dead horses,
roots of pine trees pushed through the pale curves of your ribs,
yellow blossoms flourished above you in autumn, and in winter
frost heaved your bones in the ground—old toilers, soil makers:

O Roger, Mackerel, Riley, Ned, Nellie, Chester, Lady Ghost.

Anne Sexton

CINDERELLA

You always read about it:
the plumber with twelve children
who wins the Irish Sweepstakes.
From toilets to riches.
That story.

Or the nursemaid,
some luscious sweet from Denmark
who captures the oldest son's heart.
From diapers to Dior.
That story.

Or a milkman who serves the wealthy,
eggs, cream, butter, yogurt, milk,
the white truck like an ambulance
who goes into real estate
and makes a pile.
From homogenized to martinis at lunch.

Or the charwoman
who is on the bus when it cracks up
and collects enough from the insurance.
From mops to Bonwit Teller.
That story.

Once
the wife of a rich man was on her deathbed
and she said to her daughter Cinderella:
Be devout. Be good. Then I will smile
down from heaven in the seam of a cloud.
The man took another wife who had
two daughters, pretty enough
but with hearts like blackjacks.
Cinderella was their maid.
She slept on the sooty hearth each night
and walked around looking like Al Jolson.
Her father brought presents home from town,
jewels and gowns for the other women
but the twig of a tree for Cinderella.

She planted that twig on her mother's grave
and it grew to a tree where a white dove sat.
Whenever she wished for anything the dove
would drop it like an egg upon the ground.
The bird is important, my dears, so heed him.

Next came the ball, as you all know.
It was a marriage market.
The prince was looking for a wife.
All but Cinderella were preparing
and gussying up for the big event.
Cinderella begged to go, too.
Her stepmother threw a dish of lentils
into the cinders and said: Pick them
up in an hour and you shall go.
The white dove brought all his friends;
all the warm wings of the fatherland came,
and picked up the lentils in a jiffy.
No, Cinderella, said the stepmother,
you have no clothes and cannot dance.
That's the way with stepmothers.

Cinderella went to the tree at the grave
and cried forth like a gospel singer:
Mama! Mama! My turtledove,
send me to the prince's ball!
The bird dropped down a golden dress
and delicate little gold slippers.
Rather a large package for a simple bird.
So she went. Which is no surprise.
Her stepmother and sisters didn't
recognize her without her cinder face
and the prince took her hand on the spot
and danced with no other the whole day.
As nightfall came she thought she'd better
get home. The prince walked her home
and she disappeared into the pigeon house
and although the prince took an axe and broke
it open she was gone. Back to her cinders.
These events repeated themselves for three days.
However on the third day the prince

covered the palace steps with cobbler's wax
and Cinderella's gold shoe stuck upon it.
Now he would find whom the shoe fit
and find his strange dancing girl for keeps.
He went to their house and the two sisters
were delighted because they had lovely feet.
The eldest went into a room to try the slipper on
but her big toe got in the way so she simply
sliced it off and put on the slipper.
The prince rode away with her until the white dove
told him to look at the blood pouring forth.
That is the way with amputations.
They don't just heal up like a wish.
The other sister cut off her heel
but the blood told as blood will.
The prince was getting tired.
He began to feel like a shoe salesman.
But he gave it one last try.
This time Cinderella fit into the shoe
like a love letter into its envelope.

At the wedding ceremony
the two sisters came to curry favor
and the white dove pecked their eyes out.
Two hollow spots were left
like soup spoons.

Cinderella and the prince
lived, they say, happily ever after,
like two dolls in a museum case
never bothered by diapers or dust,
never arguing over the timing of an egg,
never telling the same story twice,
never getting a middle-aged spread,
their darling smiles pasted on for eternity.
Regular Bobbsey Twins.
That story.

Walt Whitman

SONG OF MYSELF (excerpts)

[Part 1]

I celebrate myself, and sing myself,
And what I assume you shall assume,
For every atom belonging to me as good belongs to you.

I loafe and invite my soul,
I lean and loafe at my ease observing a spear of summer grass.

My tongue, every atom of my blood, form'd from this soil, this air,
Born here of parents born here from parents the same, and their
                                                    parents the same,
I, now thirty-seven years old in perfect health begin,
Hoping to cease not till death.

Creeds and schools in abeyance,
Retiring back a while sufficed at what they are, but never forgotten,
I harbor for good or bad, I permit to speak at every hazard,
Nature without check with original energy.

[from Part 2]

Have you reckon'd a thousand acres much? have you reckon'd
                                                    the earth much?
Have you practis'd so long to learn to read?
Have you felt so proud to get at the meaning of poems?

Stop this day and night with me and you shall possess the origin of
                                                    all poems,
You shall possess the good of the earth and sun, (there are millions
                                                    of suns left,)
You shall no longer take things at second or third hand, nor look
through the eyes of the dead, nor feed on the spectres in books,
You shall not look through my eyes either, nor take things from me,
You shall listen to all sides and filter them from your self.

[from part 52]

The spotted hawk swoops by and accuses me, he complains of my gab
and my loitering.

I too am not a bit tamed, I too am untranslatable,
I sound my barbaric yaws over the roofs of the world.

Recommended Books About Poetry

For Teachers and Students

Babette Deutsch, *Poetry Handbook: A Dictionary of Terms*. New York: HarperResource, 1982.

There are several editions of this book; it's easy to find a used one online.

Donald Hall, *To Read a Poem*. Stamford, CT: Heinle Publishers, 1992

John Hollander, *Rhyme's Reason*. New Haven, CT: Yale University Press, 1989.

This is a fun little book that explains different forms by writing in them, an amazing feat in itself.

Kenneth Koch and Kate Farrell, *Sleeping on the Wing: An Anthology of Modern Poetry with Essays on Reading and Writing*. New York: Vintage Books, 1982.

For Middle School and High School Teachers

David Cappella and Baron Wormser, *Teaching the Art of Poetry: The Moves*. Mahwah, NJ: Lawrence Erlbaum Publishers, 2000.

Also, there is a terrific *Conference on Poetry & Teaching* held every summer at the Frost Place in Franconia, New Hampshire. For information, visit www.frostplace.org.

Recommended Books and Links About Adoption

Books

Robert Andersen, M.D., *Second Choice: Growing Up Adopted.* O'Fallon, MO: Badger Hill Press, 1993.

Nina Bernstein, *The Lost Children of Wilder: The Epic Struggle to Change Foster Care.* New York: Vintage Books, 2002.

David M. Brodzinsky, PhD., Marshall D. Schechter, M.D., and Robin Marantz Henig, *Being Adopted: The Lifelong Search for Self.* New York: Anchor Books, 1993.

Betty Jean Lifton, *Journey of the Adopted Self.* New York: Perseus Publishing, 1995.

Karen Salyer McElmurray, *Surrendered Child: A Birth Mother's Journey.* Atlanta: University of Georgia Press, 2004.

Catherine McKinley, *The Book of Sarahs: A Memoir.* New York: Counterpoint Press, 2003.

Adam Pertman, *Adoption Nation: How the Adoption Revolution is Transforming America.* New York: Basic Books, 2001.

Mary Jo Rillera, A*doption Searchbook: Techniques for Tracing People.* Third Edition. Encinitas, CA: Pure CA (formerly Triadoption Publications), 1993

Sarah Saffin, *Ithaka: A Daughter's Memoir of Being Found.* New York: Dell Publishing Company, Inc., 1999.

Joe Soll, *Adoption Healing.* Congers, NY: Adoption Crosssroads, 2000.

Jean A. S. Strauss, *Birthright: The Guide to Search and Reunion for Adoptees, Birthparents, and Adoptive Parents.* New York: Penguin Books, 1994.

Susan Wadia-Ells, ed., *The Adoption Reader: Birth Mothers, Adoptive Mothers and Adopted Daughters Tell Their Stories.* New York: Avalon Publishing Group, 1995.

Links on the World Wide Web

www.americanadoptioncongress.com (information about adoption reform)

www.adoptees.meetup.com (find a support group near you)

www.adoptioninstitute.org (information about adoption and adoption reform)

www.adopting.org (search and support resources related to international adoptions)

www.familylifecycle.com (multicultural mental health group)

www.tapestrybooks.com (books and literature about adoption)

Acknowledgments

This book was inspired by Jacqueline Woodson's *Locomotion*, a book of poems written in the voice of an eleven-year-old boy who is in foster care. I am deeply grateful to Jackie for writing that book, and for encouraging me to write this one. Her suggestions and insights along the way were invaluable; her "you can do this" attitude kept me going.

I am also deeply thankful to Norma Fox Mazer, whose books have always inspired me. She has been a supporter and fierce advocate of this book; without her, it would probably be sitting in a drawer. I'm glad that Lizzie's poems encouraged her to experiment more with poems, too.

Thanks always goes to my husband, Mike Fleming, who is my best editor and supporter; and to Meg Dunn de Pulido, my first and best friend, who's always been there for me. Other friends who've supported me through this book and through my "adoption quests" include Catherine McKinley, Laure-Anne Bosselaar, Martha Rhodes, Robert Smith, Joe Soll, Adam Bagdasarian, Jan Beatty, Meghan Adler, Carol Hohman, and Fran Graffeo. I'd also like to extend a special acknowledgment to fellow poet Deborah Smith Bernstein, who was wonderfully enthusiastic about this book and has been supportive of my literary efforts for more than seventeen years.

I'd also like to extend a special thanks to Wendy Freund of the Adoption Unit at the New York Foundling Hospital, for her assistance, support, encouragement, and advice on so many matters—including my afterword.

I also want to acknowledge my agent, Elaine Markson, who called me and said "I love this book."

Thanks, too, to Karen Braziller and Persea Books for liking this book enough to publish it, and offering both editorial guidance and the chance to write an afterword.

In writing parts of the afterword, I checked my facts against the information found in *Adoption Nation: How the Adoption Revolution is Transforming America*, written by my friend Adam Pertman. Thanks, Adam.

Finally, I want to thank my family—both my adoptive and blood relatives, but especially my mom and dad and older sister and brother—for their constant love, support, and understanding.

About the Author

Meg Kearney was born in Manhattan and, soon after, placed into foster care under the auspices of the New York Foundling Hospital. At age five months, she lucked out: she was adopted and brought to live in a little town called LaGrange, located in New York State's Hudson Valley, 75 miles north of New York City. She grew up there with her parents; two older adopted siblings; and her best friend, also named Meg, who lived across the road.

Today, Ms. Kearney (pronounced car-nee) is the director of the Solstice Creative Writing Programs of Pine Manor College in Chestnut Hill, Massachusetts. She writes poetry for both adults and young adults, including *The Girl in the Mirror* and *When You Never Said Goodbye*, the second and third novels in the Lizzie McLane trilogy. Among her poetry books for adults are *An Unkindness of Ravens* and the award-winning volume, *Home by Now*. She has also published a critically acclaimed picture book for children, *Trouper* (illustrated by E. B. Lewis). Kearney's poems have appeared in myriad literary journals and anthologies, and have been read on Garrison Keillor's national radio show, "A Writer's Almanac."

Before she went to work for Pine Manor College, Ms. Kearney taught poetry at The New School University and was associate director of the National Book Foundation, sponsor of the National Book Awards, in New York City. Prior to that, she taught school children about electrical safety and conducted power plant tours for a gas & electric company in upstate New York.

Meg Kearney frequently visits schools and college classrooms nationwide, where she reads her poetry and discusses craft. She often is a speaker at literary and adoption conferences. She lives in New Hampshire with her husband, their three-legged dog, Trouper, and two cats, Hopkins and Magpie. Visit her website: www.megkearney.com.